Lord Mumford's Minx

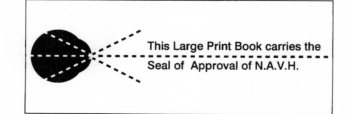

This Large Print Book carries the
Seal of Approval of N.A.V.H.

Lord Mumford's Minx

Debbie Raleigh

Thorndike Press • Waterville, Maine

Published in 2002 by arrangement with Zebra Books,
an imprint of Kensington Publishing Corp.

Thorndike Press Large Print Romance Series.

The tree indicium is a trademark of Thorndike Press.

The text of this Large Print edition is unabridged.
Other aspects of the book may vary from the original edition.

Set in 16 pt. Plantin by Al Chase.

Printed in the United States on permanent paper.

Library of Congress Cataloging-in-Publication Data
Raleigh, Debbie.
    Lord Mumford's minx / Debbie Raleigh.
       p. cm.
    ISBN 0-7862-3912-3 (lg. print : hc : alk. paper)
    1. Large type books.   I. Title.
  PS3618.A45 L67 2002
   813′.6—dc21
                                                    2001057021

Lord Mumford's Minx

One

Standing in the center of the tidy office, Miss Cassandra Stanholte glared at the small, insipid Man of Business currently cowering behind the large desk.

"What do you mean there is nothing to be done?" she demanded, her tone as commanding as her expression. "Surely you do not expect me to hand over a sizable fortune, not to mention an estate that has been in my family for five generations, to some stranger who claims to have been married to my long-lost uncle?"

Running a nervous hand over his rapidly thinning hair, Mr. Albert Carson regarded the unexpected intruder in a wary manner. Although the young maiden appeared remarkably harmless with her demure gray gown and her golden hair tugged into a haphazard knot, he was not a bit comforted. Indeed, he was uncannily disturbed by the flashing silver eyes and stubborn jut of the softly rounded chin.

"Please, Miss Stanholte, I am suggesting nothing of the kind," he retorted in what he hoped was a soothing manner, "but you must understand that I am in a very . . . delicate situation."

"And what about my position? I assure you that it is untenable."

"It is not that I do not sympathize, but as you know, Lady Stanholte has provided a certificate of marriage to your uncle as well as a birth certificate for their child. She has also provided proof of his death in India last year. Clearly, we must at least investigate her claim that her son is legal heir to the Stanholte title."

Cassie bit back a delightfully rude comment. Although Mr. Carson was no doubt doing his best, she was in no mood to listen to his evasive explanations. In the past fortnight she had endured a horde of strangers invading her home, a near revolt by her tenants, the unpleasant gossip of her neighbors and a ghastly drive from Devonshire to London. She wanted a firm promise that the odious mess would be put to a swift end. Instead it appeared that she might lose everything while this timid man fussed over false certificates and the clever lies of an obvious charlatan. Really, it was more than any woman should have to bear.

"Mr. Carson." She moved forward to place her hands on the wide desk. "My uncle disappeared on a trip to the Continent thirty years ago. After his disappearance, my grandfather spent the next ten years and a vast sum of money searching for his whereabouts. Nothing was ever found. Not a trace that he was still alive."

"Yes, I recall my father speaking of the incident. Quite tragic."

She ignored his sympathetic words. "Naturally, the estate reverted to my father, and on my parents' death, to me. Now, do you not find it in the least odd that if my uncle were indeed alive he never made any attempt to contact the family, if only to ensure that he maintained control of his rightful inheritance?"

"Oh, yes, decidedly odd." Albert cleared his throat in an uneasy manner.

"Then why haven't you notified the authorities and had this . . . woman taken from my home?"

"As I have said, Miss Stanholte, proper procedures must be followed."

The devil with proper procedures, Cassie inwardly fumed, straightening with an angry motion.

"This is absurd, Mr. Carson. Any woman could claim to have married my uncle in the past thirty years. Indeed, for all I know, I might have a dozen aunts waiting to show up on my doorstep with heirs to the Stanholte estate."

"Really, Miss Stanholte, I believe you are exaggerating the situation," Albert protested, his tone flustered.

"Am I?" Cassie arched a golden brow. "It appears to me that all a person needs are a few well-contrived lies and a marriage certificate to acquire the title of their choice."

"I assure you that I am doing everything possible to discover the veracity of this claim."

"But how can you?" she demanded, her silver eyes flashing. "According to the supposed Lady Stanholte, my uncle died after conveniently leaving her a son and a deathbed wish to have him properly raised at the family estate. He obviously is incapable of verifying or denying any such marriage. Unless, of course, you propose to dig him up."

"Yes . . . well . . ." Clearly unhinged by the upheaval in his staunchly predictable life, Albert fussed with the cravat that appeared to be choking him. "There are a number of inquiries I intend to make before anything is settled. Indeed, I have already sent correspondence to several acquaintances in India. We shall no doubt get to the truth of the matter in time."

Cassie was not appeased. It was all well and good for this man to speak of some eventual resolution of her predicament. His household had not been thrown into disarray and his servants on the point of walking out.

"I will not allow that encroacher to remain in my house while you dither over the finer points of the law," she retorted in sharp tones.

Albert lifted his hands in a helpless motion. "I am sorry, Miss Stanholte, but there is really nothing I can do."

"Then clearly I shall have to take matters into my own hands," Cassie announced, her delicate features set in lines of determination.

"Miss Stanholte, I would sternly advise against any hasty actions. This is a situation that calls for —"

"I know precisely what the situation calls for, Mr. Carson," she interrupted with a toss of her head.

Clearly sensing that Cassie was more than capable of plunging herself into disaster for the sake of family pride, Albert abruptly rose to his feet.

"You are understandably distraught, Miss Stanholte. I would suggest that you stay in London for a few days, perhaps enjoy a few of the entertainments, and then we will discuss this situation again."

Gray eyes flashed with a dangerous fire at the patronizing tone. "I have no desire to enjoy the local entertainment. All I want is that woman out of my house."

"Surely you would like to visit the shops —"

"Mr. Carson, I came to London because I assumed you would be willing to do whatever was necessary to save my estate. It seems I was mistaken," Cassie informed the incompetent attorney in stiff tones. "It is becoming increasingly obvious that I will have to deal with this unpleasant matter on my own."

"But —"

"With or without your help, I intend to prove Lady Stanholte is a fraud."

"Miss Stanholte —"

"Good day, Mr. Carson."

Without waiting to hear any more foolish arguments, Cassie turned on her heel and marched from the stuffy office.

Really, the man was impossible, she seethed as she stalked down the long hall. He should be doing whatever was necessary to safeguard her inheritance from such ghastly intruders. Instead he appeared quite content to dawdle in his office cowardly hoping the unpleasant situation would simply disappear.

Well, thankfully, she was not so hen-hearted. Although she was virtually alone in the world, she was no helpless Miss unable to protect herself from devious scoundrels. Just the opposite, in fact. She possessed far more of the Stanholte stubborn pride and fiery temperament than was reasonably proper for a young lady.

Why should she be forced to hand over her estate just because she was a woman on her own? If her father were alive, he would certainly be prepared to go to any length to protect his inheritance. Why should she be any different?

No, she thought grimly, she would not concede defeat. The estate was all she had left of her parents. She would fight to the bitter end to protect what they had left entrusted to her care. And with the letter she had tucked in a pocket of her cloak, she knew precisely where to begin her search.

Halting in the small hallway, Cassie withdrew the crumpled note. She had discovered the letter hidden in the belongings of Lady Stanholte shortly after her arrival in Devonshire. At the time, she had felt a pang of remorse at prying through the lady's private correspondence. Now she could only be relieved that she had put aside her finer sensibilities.

Unfolding the cheap parchment, Cassie held it up. In the dim lighting, the scrawled words were nearly impossible to decipher, but after studying them for the past fortnight, Cassie could recite them by heart.

Liza,

I know how yer said not to rite, but I must beg yer to give up this daft notion. No good can come of trying to rise abuv yer station, and I fear yer be as likely to end up in the cove as to be Lady Stanholte.

I have left the stage as Herbie has at last put me in a proper establishment. T'aint much as Herbie is as skinflinted as he is dimwitted, but there is room enuf for yer to stay until yer gets yerself on yer feet.

Nell

The letter convinced her beyond a shadow of a doubt that Lady Stanholte was nothing more than a common thief, and that this Nell was well aware of the plot to steal Cassie's inheritance.

All Cassie needed to do was locate the woman and force her to reveal the truth.

Simple enough.

But first she would have to acquire the courage to enter the most notorious neighborhood in all of London.

14

★ ★ ★

"Egad, Mumford, has your coachman gone soft in the noodle?" Leaning forward to peer out of the window, Lord Horatio Bidwell wrinkled his distinctly pointed nose. "He's clearly taken a wrong turn."

Seated across from the thin, flamboyantly attired gentleman, Luke Travell, Earl of Mumford, allowed a small smile to touch his handsome countenance.

"Rest assured, Biddles, my coachman possesses full control of his faculties," he drawled, his magnificent blue eyes glinting with humor. "I requested him to make a brief halt before we go on to White's."

"A halt? In this neighborhood?" With a dramatic shudder, Biddles threw himself back in his seat to regard his companion in a petulant fashion. "Why the devil didn't you warn me? I would never have agreed to accompany you if I had realized your intention."

"My business will take but a moment. And there is nothing amiss with this neighborhood. Indeed, it is quite proper."

"Precisely my point," Biddles complained with a disdainful sniff. "The place utterly reeks of respectability. Imagine the damage to my reputation if I am seen."

Luke chuckled. It was true that Lord

15

Bidwell took great pains to cultivate a frivolous image. Few among society considered him more than a twittering fool, renowned for his outrageous behavior and decidedly cutting tongue. Luke, however, was well aware that it was a dangerous mistake to underestimate the man's formidable intelligence. Like himself, Lord Bidwell was often recruited by the War Office to perform the more delicate assignments. Assignments that needed the utmost secrecy.

Unfortunately, Luke's own brilliant career had come to an abrupt end several months before. Much to his annoyance, the unexpected death of a distant cousin had encumbered him with a ponderous fortune and a vast estate that required a tedious amount of attention. His carefree days of daring adventures were now only a fond memory, replaced by days spent closeted with estate managers, investment bankers and long-neglected tenants. Even when he managed to escape to London there seemed an endless number of details that required his personal attention, and, of course, the dreary round of social obligations his position made impossible to decline.

"I am confident your reputation will survive a passing brush with respectability, Biddles," Luke consoled his sulking companion, determinedly shoving aside his brief flare of self-pity. It seemed rather ludicrous to regret what most would consider a stroke of incredible fortune. Even if he did at times feel as if a noose had been slipped about his neck. "But, of course, if you are concerned, you could always huddle on the floor until we leave."

"And risk ruining this exquisite attire?" Biddles demanded in horror, glancing down at the claret coat that provided a shocking contrast to his pink waistcoat. "Don't be absurd. This delightful ensemble cost me a small fortune."

Luke quirked a raven brow. "You can't mean to say that you were actually asked to pay for that ghastly insult to fashion?"

"I say, most unsporting of you, Luke," Biddles protested, his expression wounded. "You have besmirched the honor of my tailor. Luckily for you, the nasty little man has been pestering me for weeks about some beastly bill or I should demand a duel."

Luke merely smiled. Unlike the clothes of his dapper friend, his own pale blue coat and buff pantaloons were cut to enhance rather than distract from his powerful frame. It was a style that was unfortunately gaining appeal among the young dandies, most of whom could not claim such a well-proportioned physique.

"I must say I am deeply relieved. You are a notoriously poor aim, and I should no doubt be forced to stand in some muddy field for hours waiting for you to draw blood."

"Perhaps." Biddles shrugged with the nonchalance of a man confident in his skill as a marksman. "But I cannot imagine it would be any more tedious than being cloistered with some stiff-rumped agent as he prattles about the wisdom of investing in barley rather than wheat or the disastrous effects of the latest labor unrest on the price of corn."

"Unfortunately, it is my duty to ensure that the family fortune isn't being dwindled away on absurd inventions or worthless gold mines." Luke grimaced, inwardly acknowledging that the staunchly proper Man of Business would be as likely to toss himself into the Thames as to take an unnecessary risk.

"Well, it is a devilish bore, if you ask me."

"Ah, yes, quite dull when compared to your habit of constantly attempting to outrun the constable."

"It adds a decided spice to life," Biddles sniffed, abruptly raising his quizzing glass as a carriage rolled past. "Egad, was that

Pembroke? Do you suppose he recognized me?"

"I fail to see how he could not have recognized you," Luke drawled with a pointed glance at the painful waistcoat. "Who else in London would be similarly attired?"

The long nose twitched, but before Biddles could conjure a suitable retort, the carriage swerved to an abrupt halt, throwing both occupants sharply against the padded walls. It took a moment for Luke to regain his scattered wits; then with years of training rushing to his aid, he found his balance and was leaping onto the crowded street with the innate grace of a natural sportsman.

Spotting his groom at the head of the perfectly matched grays, Luke hurried forward, quite prepared to discover that the street had crumbled into oblivion. That could be the only reasonable excuse for his groom's cowhanded treatment of his thoroughbreds. What he found instead was a tiny bundle of gray topped by a mass of golden curls lying at his groom's feet.

"What the devil . . . ? Jameson, what is about?"

Hearing his approach, the young groom turned to gaze at him with fearful eyes, clearly shaken by the small form huddled in the street.

"I'm sorry, my lord, but the young lady stepped directly in me path. I did me best. Honest I did. But . . . Oh, blimey, it t'wasn't my fault. It t'wasn't."

Realizing the groom was swiftly working himself into a pucker, Luke regarded him in a stern manner.

"Go fetch the carriage blanket, Jameson."

"I . . . Yes, my lord."

Scurrying back to the carriage, the groom left Luke alone to carefully round the skittish grays and slowly kneel beside the recumbent young lady. Then with exquisite care he turned her onto her back.

Just for a moment he felt his breath catch in his throat. How tiny she was, he thought inanely. Like a delicate child laid down for a nap. Rather hesitantly he reached out to push aside her cloud of silken curls. An odd pang twisted in his heart at the pale oval face that appeared so utterly still. He could see no obvious sign of injuries, but he knew that was no reassurance that she had not received grievous wounds in the unfortunate accident.

Almost unconsciously his slender fingers moved to gently wipe a smudge of dust from her smooth cheek. He knew that he would never forgive himself if she were to die, regardless of the fact he had no way of preventing the grim situation. Then a flare of deep relief rushed through his body as the long, black lashes began to flutter.

"No, do not move," he urged as she began to lift herself off the hard pavement, his hands instinctively grasping her shoulders.

Turning her head, she regarded him with bewildered silver eyes, blinking rapidly as if startled by the sight of his dark, aquiline face so close to her own.

"What . . . What has occurred?" she asked softly, her cultured voice at considerable odds with the ragtag gown.

"I fear you had a rather nasty fall."

"A fall?"

"Yes. You apparently stepped in front of my carriage."

"Did I?"

"According to my distinctly distraught groom."

"Oh." She considered his words a long moment; then a shudder shook through her slender frame. "Yes, I remember."

"Are you injured?"

"No, I do not think so," she responded cautiously.

Luke frowned. "Are you quite certain?"

Without warning, a thoroughly charming dimple danced beside the inviting mouth. "Not unless you count my pride,

21

which I must admit has taken a decided beating."

The smile had a distinctly disturbing effect on Luke. From a man solely concerned with a young damsel in dire distress, he was suddenly aware that she was quite lovely despite her current dishabille.

Certainly not a beauty in the traditional sense, he acknowledged with his usual honesty. The chin was too firm, the mouth a bit too generous, and the fine gray eyes more shrewd than tempting, but even for a man accustomed to women devoting endless hours to their appearance, he had to admit there was something very compelling about the delicate countenance.

His frank appraisal might have continued for several more moments, but a delightful flood of color suddenly stained her pale skin, revealing that she was not so rattled that she had missed his admiring glance. With an effort, he attempted to ignore the faint scent of violets that drifted from her glorious golden curls, and the warmth of her skin he could feel beneath the thin fabric of her gown.

"Perhaps I should send for a physician. I would feel easier of spirit to be assured that nothing is amiss."

"I am quite fine."

"Still, it cannot do harm to have him take a look."

"Oh, no, please," she protested, an undeniable plea in the dove gray eyes. "I have made enough of a spectacle of myself as it is. I just wish to go to my carriage."

For a man who made it a strict habit never to spend a moment longer in the company of a young, eligible lady than absolutely necessary, Luke was oddly reluctant to allow the young chit to slip into obscurity. Indeed, he felt his hands tightening as if afraid she might simply disappear in a puff of smoke.

"Nonsense," he heard himself saying. "I shall take you home myself. I assume you have an establishment in London?"

His generous offer had an odd effect on the young maiden as a guarded expression descended on her pale features.

"You are very kind, but I assure you that is not necessary. Indeed, I have no need of any further assistance."

He blinked, distinctly caught off guard by her lack of enthusiasm. Really, the chit seemed thoroughly indifferent to the fact that any number of women would be swooning with delight to be in her current position.

"Perhaps not, but imagine what a cad I

should be painted if I did not fulfill my duty as a gentleman," he perversely insisted, unaccustomed to such a nonchalant dismissal.

A reluctant smile twitched at the enticing lips, the enchanting dimples once more dancing to life. "I don't think you care a fig what others think of you," she retorted shrewdly.

Luke couldn't prevent a boyish grin. "No, but I do detest my man of affairs," he cajoled. "This provides a most admirable excuse to fob him off yet again."

"I fear you shall have to devise another means of eluding your man of affairs, sir."

"And why should I?" he demanded, the raven head tilting to one side. "This is clearly the best solution to a very unpleasant episode."

"I would simply prefer the comfort of my own carriage —"

The chiding words were suddenly interrupted as Biddles made an untimely entrance into the scene, his quizzing glass raised to inspect Luke's rather suggestive hold on the young maiden.

"Egad, Mumford, not another damsel throwing herself at your indifferent feet?" the man drawled. "I believe she is the third today, is she not?"

For once Luke found little amusement in

his friend's droll sense of humor, and quite clearly the young damsel found even less as she jerked away from his restraining hold and scrambled hastily to her feet. Then, with only the briefest attempt to smooth the gown that had not improved with its intimate acquaintance with the soggy pavement, she lifted her head to regard the small man with a dangerous intensity.

"Pardon me?"

"I was simply pointing out that you happen to be the third young maiden to toss yourself at my friend's feet today," Biddles obligingly repeated.

"Toss myself at his feet?"

Ignoring Luke's thunderous scowl, Biddles waved a hand in a dismissive motion.

"But of course, my dear. It is quite shocking, the lengths to which young chits will go to capture the fancy of the Irresistible Earl." Biddles gave a small laugh. "But then, I don't have to tell you that, do I?"

"Of all the . . . If you believe for one moment that I would be willing to risk my life to gain the attention of a . . . a mere man, then you are sadly mistaken." The woman jutted her chin to a disdainful angle, the eyes flashing silver fury. "In fact, sir, you belong in Bedlam."

Wishing Biddles were indeed in Bedlam, Luke made an effort to repair the damage.

"I believe my companion is making a poor attempt at a jest."

"Am I?" Blinking in mock surprise, Biddles tapped his quizzing glass against his forehead. "Somehow I seem to recall you bemoaning the devious debutantes who were incessantly twisting their ankles or stumbling sideways just as you passed. Now, where do you suppose I came up with such an odd fancy?"

A deadly silence fell as the young woman turned to regard Luke as if he belonged in one of the nearby gutters.

"I was mistaken," she retorted between clenched teeth. "You both belong in Bedlam. Good day, sirs."

With a dismissive toss of her golden head, the young lady turned with military precision and began marching up the busy street. Immediately, Luke was in her wake, determined to at least apologize for his companion's unfortunate remarks. But as if fate were on her side, an impatient tilbury swerved past the halted carriage, forcing Luke to jump aside or be run down. Annoyingly, the woman was lost in the crowd by the time the ill-mannered driver had passed.

Not certain why he felt such a surge of

frustration at the thought that he might never see the golden-haired beauty again, Luke turned to glare at his friend with obvious irritation.

"Perhaps you would be so good as to explain that bit of nonsense, Biddles?"

The small man gave an offended sniff of his nose. "Really, Mumford, I wish you would decide whether you desire to be rescued from the ploys of cunning females or not. I would just as soon have remained in the carriage. Pembroke is bound to have noticed me by now."

"I hardly think any female, no matter how cunning, would be willing to fling herself beneath a carriage," Luke pointed out in dry tones.

A knowing glint entered the piercing brown eyes. "I was not referring to her manner of halting the carriage, Mumford, which was no doubt nothing more than a fortunate accident, but rather her ability to hold you spellbound on a decidedly damp street."

"Hardly spellbound, Biddles," Luke denied, refusing to admit that he had not even noticed the street was damp. "More . . . intrigued."

"Indeed?" Biddles replied with obvious disbelief.

A renegade smile abruptly curved the surprisingly full lips as Luke glanced up the street. Perhaps he had been more than a bit intrigued by the lovely woman, he reluctantly conceded.

"You know, Biddles," he softly mused, "I have never noted how decidedly partial I am to the scent of violets."

Two

For what seemed the hundredth time, Cassie glanced through the letter she had discovered hidden in Lady Stanholte's trunk. And for the hundredth time she ended up shaking her head in frustration.

Clearly, there was no further information to be gained within the nearly unintelligible note. Nothing beyond the fact that the woman who had arrived on her doorstep a fortnight ago, carrying a small boy and a message from her solicitor that she was to be given entrance to the Stanholte estate, possessed the first name of Liza, and that she was acquainted with a former actress named Nell. She also knew that Nell was now comfortably established in a home rented by a clutch-fisted Herbie. But what had seemed such a simple task in Devonshire was proving to be devilishly difficult.

Of course, she acknowledged wryly, she had been thoroughly unacquainted with the peculiar nature of courtesans when she had been in Devonshire. Like most delicately reared ladies, she had been only vaguely acquainted with the scandalous tales of fallen women. She had simply assumed that within days, if not hours, of renting an establishment in the notorious neighborhood she would have stumbled across Nell. And of course, once she had found Nell it would be only a matter of discovering the proper method of convincing her to admit that her friend Liza had never been acquainted with the missing Lord Stanholte, let alone his wife. It had never occurred to her that the inhabitants of the neighborhood would so zealously guard their privacy, or that they would bluntly refuse to admit they had even heard of any actress named Nell or her mysterious friend named Liza.

Now it appeared that she would have to consider a new approach to her dilemma. One that was even more daring than renting a home in such a neighborhood.

Abruptly rising to her feet, Cassie crossed the small bedroom to peer at herself in the oval mirror. At least no one was likely to recognize her, she acknowledged with a rather distasteful grimace. Gone was the distinctly shabby maiden that had arrived in London three days before, and in her place was an elegant courtesan with curls darkened to a brilliant shade of red and artfully arranged about the carefully painted face. Even the gray dress had been discarded in favor of a jade green gown that revealed a startling amount of pale skin. A more than adequate disguise, considering that no one in London was remotely acquainted with her beyond her Man of Business.

Unless, of course, one counted the Irresistible Earl . . .

Her grimace only deepened at the renegade notion. For three days she had attempted to put aside all thoughts of the dark-haired stranger that had witnessed her folly. After all, there was nothing notable about the incident beyond the fact she had made a perfect fool of herself by wandering onto the busy street like the worst sort of greenhorn.

But while she could sternly tell herself the Irresistible Earl was nothing more than a puffed-up cully, she found it annoyingly difficult to dismiss the memory of the magnificently handsome countenance and wicked blue eyes. More than once she had found her attention straying back to their brief encounter, recalling his captivating smile and seemingly genuine concern for her welfare. She even remembered the feel of his warm hands as they pressed against her shoulders.

Which only proved that she could be as much a sapskull as the next woman, she told herself severely. It was clear the odious earl was a self-opinionated bore who imagined every woman throughout England was wilting to capture his jaded attention. She could only assume the nasty spill had rattled her usual wits to the point of insensibility.

Rather pleased with the logical explanation for her absurd reaction to the Irresistible Earl, Cassie absently tugged at the scandalous neckline of her diaphanous gown, wondering if perhaps she could add a shawl without too much comment, when the door to her bedroom was abruptly thrust open to reveal a large, silver-haired woman with a dour expression.

"Well, I see that you are bound and determined to land us in a bumblebath, Miss Cassie," the housekeeper chided, her disapproving gaze sweeping over the daring gown.

Cassie heaved a rueful sigh. She had been expecting this encounter since she had ordered the carriage to be sent round. Mary Green had been with the Stanholte family since Cassie was a small child, and rarely missed an opportunity to speak her mind. Still, Cassie did her best to avert the severe scolding that was no doubt in the offing.

"Please, Mary, there is no need to cause a fuss."

"Indeed?" Mary placed her hands on her ample hips. "Bad enough that you came to

London without a proper chaperon, and then rented an establishment in a neighborhood that is fit only for . . . for . . ."

"I believe they are referred to as Cyprians," Cassie couldn't resist supplying with a mock innocent expression. Her efforts were received with a stern frown.

"And now you brazenly appear in public where anyone might recognize you. Well, it is certainly a comfort that your poor mother is not here to see you; that is all I can say."

"Actually, I have a feeling there is a great deal more you could say," Cassie retorted with a rather weary smile. "But not now, I beg of you."

The frown deepened, but this time with concern. "Has something occurred?"

"No, and that is precisely the problem," Cassie revealed, restlessly pacing toward the window that offered a view of the surrounding neighborhood. "I was so certain when I found that letter that it would be a simple matter to discover the truth. After all, there can not be an overabundance of actresses named Nell who are under the protection of a man named Herbie. But thus far I have done little more than waste my time."

"I fear I have done little better with the servants," Mary admitted, her expression one of disgust. "A pretty lot of snobs they are, walking about with their fine London airs. They haven't the least interest in sharing a nice, homey coz."

Cassie flashed the older woman a sympathetic glance. Although Mary had disapproved of the scheme from the start, Cassie knew that she would do everything in her power to help her. She was the one ally that Cassie knew she could always depend upon.

"I would think it more prudence than London airs, Mary. It appears the least said, the better in this neighborhood. No doubt a misplaced word could create a most unpleasant scandal or even put an end to a courtesan's favorable connection. It is a difficulty that I must admit I had not anticipated."

Mary heaved a visible sigh of relief. "Then you are giving up on this daft notion?"

"Certainly not." Tossing her vibrant curls, Cassie stiffened her back with a determined motion. It was a sight that made the housekeeper's heart sink. "I have simply concluded that I cannot confine myself to this house. Our neighbors may be unwilling to speak of this mysterious Nell, but I am quite certain that her acquaintances at the theater will be more forthcoming. And of course, there is bound to be one gentleman among the London *ton* who will recognize the name of Herbie. Which is precisely why I must make a public appearance in the park today."

Far from appeased, Mary shook her head in an accusing manner. "It is positively disgraceful. Young ladies do not appear in public without a proper chaperon and dressed in such a vulgar manner."

"Perhaps not, but it is either this or returning to Devonshire and the current Lady Stanholte," Cassie pointed out with a decided lack of patience. "I suppose if you are quite fortunate, she may be willing to offer you a position."

"That will be enough of your sass, child," Mary retorted with a wounded sniff. "I have no intention of working for that impostor."

Instantly contrite, Cassie swiftly crossed the room to give the woman a consoling hug.

"Oh, I am sorry, Mary, but I fear I am sadly out of temper. I just wish this was all behind us."

"As do I, child," Mary admitted, no more immune to Cassie's generous nature than anyone else. "It was an evil day when that woman darkened the door. An evil day indeed."

"Well, if luck be on our side, Mary, she will soon be darkening the door of Newgate. All I need is to find Nell and all our troubles will be behind us."

Mary was not nearly so convinced. She knew quite well that any woman acquainted with London could easily lose herself in the vast crowd. Indeed, this Nell might be hidden anywhere. But for once she held her tongue. It was bad enough that her stubborn mistress was determined to shred her reputation beyond repair. At least she would be safe enough in Hyde Park. It would be quite another story should she take it in her head to poke through the dens of iniquity that ran rampant throughout the city.

"As you say, Miss Cassie, all our troubles will be behind us."

Despite their tardy arrival, the two gentlemen currently entering the park attracted a great deal of attention. Indeed, it would be difficult not to note the slender man with a striped orange waistcoat and emerald green coat. Lord Bidwell always managed to command a good deal of speculation with his outrageous attire, as well as more than a few snide comments, although they were always muttered in a low voice, since the gentleman in question was remarkable in his ability to make one appear a fool. But the center of interest was on Lord Mumford, who appeared astonishingly handsome in a dark blue coat and pantaloons tucked into a pair of gleaming Hessians.

Not surprisingly, he commanded his own share of snide comments due to the fact most gentlemen found it utterly galling that a man blessed with title and fortune should also possess a handsome countenance and athletic form. Women, on the other hand, instinctively sat a bit straighter and pinched their pale cheeks on the off chance the Irresistible Earl might be gracious enough to glance in their direction.

Unfortunately for them, Lord Mumford was thoroughly indifferent to the elegant crowd that filled the park. In fact, he had only agreed to the outing since Biddles had purchased a new Bit of Calvary he was determined to parade at the fashionable hour. And, of course, it served as a means of passing a tedious afternoon.

A wry smile touched his firm lips. What he needed, he decided, was another golden-haired beauty tossing herself in his path. She at least had added a dash of excitement to his day, and oddly filled more than one dull moment with the memory of her willful gray eyes and sweet smile. And although he would never admit as much, there was rarely a day he hadn't searched the crowded streets for a glimpse of the delicate profile.

Annoyingly, it appeared he was doomed to failure. No one had seen or heard of the elusive young woman with golden hair and silver eyes. She clearly had disappeared without a trace.

Raising a languid hand to stifle a yawn, Luke glanced at his companion, who was busily quizzing the various occupants of the park. Unlike himself, Biddles found a vast deal of amusement in watching the elegant crowd.

"Ah . . . I see that Lady Howell has managed to wrangle a new carriage from her latest *chérie amie*, quite a bang-up rig, although those bays are a queer lot if I don't miss my guess. And there is Newly, back from his excursion to the country. No doubt his dragon of a grandmother handed over the sizable fortune needed to haul him out of dun territory just to rid herself of his presence, a tedious toadeater if I ever met one. And there is Umbridge, as hideously attired as ever. I do believe his sizable posterior has grown even larger over the past winter. Oh, and of course, Lady Steldon, poor creature. One would think that Lord Steldon would be good enough to stick his spoon in the wall once they were wed — he is, after all, fifty years her senior — but I suppose he is too clutch-fisted to turn up his toes and allow his despairing wife the pleasure of his inheritance . . . Oh, I say, have a look, Mumford."

Barely noting the ramblings of his companion, Luke reluctantly turned his head to regard what had captured Biddle's attention. It took him a moment to spot the cream-colored carriage sporting a young lady with brilliant red curls and a decidedly provocative gown. Certainly a beauty, he concluded, and presumably new to London since he had yet to encounter the lovely Impure. But that did not explain his friend's obvious interest.

"Prime bit of muslin," he drawled, "but I thought you had a decided preference for dark-haired beauties."

The long nose twitched as Biddles glanced at him in a mocking fashion.

"Do you not find her in the least familiar?"

Lifting his quizzing glass, Luke once more studied the woman, his blue eyes narrowing as she turned her head to reveal a delicate nose and firm jaw. An elusive memory seemed to flicker to life, but for once he discovered himself unable to pin down the precise image. Quite annoying for a man who had once lived on his sheer wits alone. He could only conclude that his luxurious way of life was making him soft in the noodle.

"There is something . . . Damn, but I must be nearing my dotage to have forgotten where I encountered such a tantalizing Venus," he retorted, his tone a shade ill-humored. "Next I suppose I shall be tottering about with swollen joints and partaking of those vile waters."

Biddles appeared smugly amused by his irritation, even going so far as to send him a consoling smile.

"Before you retire to Bath, old chap, it might interest you to know that I make a habit of never forgetting a face. It is quite distressing how easily people can be fooled by a change of clothing. Why, a clever bloke suitably attired could no doubt serve Napoleon a brandy in his own bed."

Although the words were tossed out in an offhand manner, Luke felt his annoyance easing as a wry smile replaced his frown. He had no doubt the little rat had managed to use the disguise of a loyal French servant — he had donned the disguise himself on more than one occasion — and he was just brazen enough to thrust his way into Napoleon's reclusive presence. That didn't, however, explain how he was acquainted with the red-haired doxy.

"No doubt, Biddles, but while I hold your undoubted skills in the highest esteem, I fail to comprehend what they have to do with the delightful Cyprian."

The air of smug satisfaction only deepened. "Perhaps it will aid your faulty memory to know that on the last occasion you encountered the delightful Cyprian she possessed golden curls and was covered in muck."

Just for a moment, Luke assumed that his friend was becoming a bit noddy. After all, the elegant courtesan had nothing in common with the innocent maiden he had found lying in the street.

But even as the thoughts passed through his mind, the woman in the carriage gave a familiar toss of her head, and Luke felt his heart give an odd leap of excitement. How could he have been so blind? Even with the change in hair color and dress, he should have known the moment he had caught sight of the sweetly carved profile. He had, after all, imagined it enough over the past three days. Thank goodness Biddles had not allowed his own wits to become flabby with disuse, he thought with a flicker of self-disgust.

"Good Lord . . ." He breathed softly. "I do believe you are right, Biddles."

"Naturally," Biddles drawled, carefully watching as the carriage approached. "I must say, I approve of the transformation."

Frowning, Luke allowed his gaze to take in the rather daring gown that revealed far more than a demure young lady considered proper.

"What the devil is the chit up to?" he murmured, as much to himself as to his companion.

Arching his brows, Biddles regarded him with wicked amusement.

"I should think you are nearer the schoolroom than your dotage if you are forced to ask such a painfully obvious question."

Luke felt a decided surge of irritation at the suggestive words. Odd, considering that he should be pleased with the notion that he could further his acquaintance with the young lady without concern about unwelcome expectations.

"I cannot credit it," he retorted in firm tones. "Although our meeting was brief, I have no doubt she is a lady of quality."

"Even ladies of quality can fall upon hard times, Mumford. Indeed, I have no doubt the back streets of London are littered with such women. And since I can consider no more dismal future than being governess to a pack of squalling brats, or even worse, saddled with a vicious tabby, I cannot say that I wholly condemn her choice."

"Perhaps." Far from convinced, Luke abruptly moved his mount forward. "Come along."

Without waiting for Biddles to respond, Luke angled his way toward the passing carriage, coming up from behind so that he could casually lean sideways to snatch the small fan off the seat without being noticed. Then with commendable skill he swerved his bay directly in the path of the carriage so that it had little choice but to come to an abrupt halt. The woman glanced upward, her face growing pale at the sight of his charming smile.

"Pardon me, but I believe this belongs to you." Luke performed an elegant bow, leaning forward to hand the stunned lady her fan.

She gazed blankly at the lacy confection, clearly too rattled by his sudden appearance to wonder how the fan had managed to come into his possession.

"I . . ." Swallowing with difficulty, she held out a reluctant hand. "Thank you."

His blue eyes glinted with devilish amusement. "I am always delighted to be of service to such a remarkably beautiful woman. Or had you forgotten?"

"Forgotten?" The teasing words seemed to clear her scattered wits, and much to Luke's surprise, a decidedly icy expression hardened the delicate features. "I fear I haven't the least notion what you mean."

"I was referring to the last occasion that we met."

Auburn brows arched in a haughty motion. "You must be mistaken, sir. We have never met before."

Not precisely a vain man, Luke nevertheless was accustomed to women who appeared suitably enraptured by his presence. In truth, he had become rather jaded by the knowledge he could take his pick of the most toasted beauties. But for the second occasion the mysterious woman appeared remarkably indifferent to the honor he was bestowing upon her. Even going so far as to deny even being acquainted. Hardly the expected behavior of a demi-rep on the search for a protector.

"Indeed?" Luke questioned, his curiosity thoroughly aroused.

"Now, if you will excuse me . . ."

Having the previous experience of her

abrupt departure, Luke was quite prepared as the carriage lurched forward. Maneuvering his mount forward, he ensured that the carriage halt or risk a collision.

"Not before I've made my deepest apologies," he retorted in smooth tones, willing to follow her lead for the moment. If she wished to pretend they had never encountered one another, then so be it. Allowing his gaze to roam appreciatively over her slender form and provocative red curls, he smiled in an inviting manner. "It is unforgivable that I should imply there is another woman in town who could hold a candle to your unsurpassable beauty. On closer inspection, I see you possess only the most passing resemblance."

A dark stain of color rushed to her cheeks at his blatant survey, even as her gray eyes flashed with a spark of irritation.

"It does not signify in the least," she retorted.

"At least the momentary confusion has given me the opportunity to introduce myself," Luke insisted, reaching out to firmly grasp her tiny fingers and raise them to his lips. Even beneath the thin gloves he could feel the leap of her pulse as her eyes widened with shock at his bold behavior. "Lord Mumford, at your service. And this rather disreputable coxcomb is Lord Bidwell."

Taking his cue, Biddles urged his own mount closer, bending forward and waving his arm in an elaborate bow.

"Enchanted, my dear, simply enchanted."

Still clasping the woman's fingers despite her less than subtle attempts to free herself from his grip, Luke regarded the lovely face with an expectant expression.

"And you are . . . ?"

Clearly wishing she possessed the nerve to plant him a facer, the woman reluctantly gave into her ingrained manners.

"Lady Greer," she supplied in clipped tones.

Luke hid a smile. If this woman was Lady Greer, then he was Napoleon Bonaparte.

"Are you recently arrived in London?"

"Yes."

Hardly informative, but the woman clearly underestimated the skill of Lord Bidwell's ear.

"From Devonshire, I would hazard," he drawled.

She stiffened, but with a commendable effort, her expression remained aloof.

"Not at all," she lied smoothly. "Actually,

I come from Ireland."

"Ireland?" Luke regarded the delicate features intently. "That is a considerable way from London. Are you here visiting or simply enjoying the sights?"

"I hardly think my reasons for traveling to London can be of interest to you, Lord Mumford."

Luke smiled in a wicked manner. "Everything about you is of interest to me, Lady Greer."

She sucked in a shocked breath at his blatant words; then, snatching her hand free, she reached up to tug impatiently on the arm of her groom.

"Drive on."

This time there was no ignoring the imperative command, and giving a jerk of the reins, the groom urged the rented nags forward, clearly indifferent to Luke's exquisite mount. Unwilling to risk injury to his horse, Luke reluctantly pulled aside, watching the retreating carriage with a narrowed gaze.

"A rather chilly reception for a young lady hoping to attract the attention of a rich benefactor, wouldn't you say, Biddles?" he murmured, still able to smell the scent of violets in the air.

"Positively frigid," the small man agreed,

his nose twitching.

"Odd." Luke cocked his raven head to one side. "Almost as odd as her refusal to recall our initial meeting."

"Clearly, she has no desire to be recognized as a golden-haired maiden with rather questionable taste in fashion and who has recently arrived from Devonshire."

"The question is, why?" Turning, Luke regarded his friend with glittering blue eyes. "Does she fear scandal for her family? Or is she hiding something more devious?"

Biddles grimaced. "Does it really matter?"

"It will enliven a decidedly dull season," Luke tossed out in an offhand manner, although there was nothing offhand about his mounting interest. "Shall we follow the intriguing Lady Greer, Biddles?"

"Do I have a choice?"

"None whatsoever."

Heaving a rueful sigh, Biddles reached beneath his coat to produce a dainty lace fan, a rather sly gleam in his eye.

"Then I suppose we shall have need of this."

Luke gave a pleased laugh at his devious friend's clever ploy. Not even he had noticed Biddles retrieve the fan from the carriage.

"You are a wicked, wicked man, Biddles," Luke congratulated.

Biddles gave a mocking bow. "I do my best."

Three

Of all the rotten luck. Restlessly pacing across the hideous salon, Cassie seethed at her futile afternoon. It was bad enough to endure the leering glances from the numerous gentlemen that had approached her carriage, none of whom claimed any knowledge of Herbie, but to actually encounter the Irresistible Earl just as she was leaving the park seemed the height of ill fortune.

Really, the man was proving to be a devilish nuisance, she thought with a flare of irritation. She had almost swooned when he had suddenly appeared, the startling blue eyes dancing with wicked amusement. Why couldn't he simply leave her in peace? After all, he supposedly avoided young ladies like the plague.

But of course, she suddenly acknowledged, he no longer considered her a young lady. Instead, she had managed to convince him that she was the type of woman who would welcome the attentions of wealthy gentlemen without the fuss of proper behavior.

Her stomach twisted in a queer manner at the thought, almost as if she actually cared what the arrogant Lord Mumford thought of her reputation. Which was ridiculous. No doubt it was merely her conscience rebelling at her reprehensible behavior, she swiftly reassured herself. Instead of fretting over the fact he considered her a common trollop, she should be congratulating herself on the fact she had managed to convince him that she had no connection with the shabby maiden he had nearly run down three days before.

The stern chiding did little to relieve the unease that had settled in the pit of her stomach. It was clear that the day's events had rattled her composure more than she had realized. What she needed, she decided with a sigh, was a soothing cup of tea.

Moving toward the bell that would summon her housekeeper, Cassie was abruptly halted as the salon door was pushed open to reveal the granite-faced butler that had come with the house staff. It was the first occasion he had sought out her company, and she regarded him in wary surprise.

"Yes, Tolson?"

With the regal dignity peculiar to London butlers, the man regarded her in a steady fashion. "A Lord Bidwell and Lord Mumford to see you, my lady," he an-

nounced, not seeming to find anything remotely unusual about her receiving two
gentlemen visitors.

Cassie gasped, too shocked to hide her
dismay from the watchful servant. Not that
he revealed any surprise by her reaction. He
looked as if the house could fall about his
ears without his blinking a well-trained eye.

"Tell them I . . . I am not receiving guests
this afternoon," she stammered, her heart
lodged directly in the middle of her throat.

"Very well, my lady." The butler bowed
his gray head and smoothly left the room.

Unconsciously twisting the thin fabric of
her jade gown, Cassie carefully listened for
the sound of retreating footsteps. How on
earth had Lord Mumford traced her to this
house? Surely she hadn't mentioned where
she lived? No, of course she hadn't, she reassured herself. The only way he could possibly have located her was if he had followed
her from the park.

The devil take the persistent man, she silently fumed.

"Stand aside. I have most urgent business." The unmistakable sound of Lord
Bidwell's voice floated through the open
door, making Cassie stiffen with dread.

"But, my lord —"

The butler's low words were drowned out

by the sound of determined footsteps, and before she could think to hide behind the heavy curtains, Lord Bidwell had swept into the room, closely followed by the disturbing Lord Mumford.

"Ah, Lady Greer, what a charming picture you present." Lord Bidwell performed a sweeping bow, his brown eyes glinting at the sight of her rigid form standing in the center of the room.

Deeply regretting the fact she did not have a pistol handy, Cassie was forced to display at least a semblance of courtesy.

"Lord Bidwell," she retorted stiffly, then, turning, she flashed the raven-haired earl an equally icy glance. "Lord Mumford."

Undaunted by her overt lack of welcome, Lord Bidwell grinned in an impudent manner.

"Frightfully sorry to inconvenience you, and all that," he said, "but after you left the park, I noted that you had dropped your fan."

She couldn't hide her start of surprise. "My fan?"

"Indeed, my dear." Moving forward, the tiny man held out the fragile bit of lace. "You really must keep a closer grip on your delightful fallals."

Closer grip indeed, she silently fumed.

The man had clearly stolen the fan while she was being distracted by his annoying companion. Reaching out her hand, Cassie snatched the fan and eyed her guest with open suspicion.

"So I am beginning to realize."

"It would be a shame to lose such a lovely object."

Wondering if the tiny man would be smiling so smugly if she decided to whack the pointed nose with her lovely object, Cassie was distracted by the discreet cough of her butler.

"Shall I have tea served, my lady?"

"No, thank you, Tolson," Cassie stated emphatically, only to be outmaneuvered by the flamboyantly attired gentleman.

"Superb suggestion, Tolson. Quite brilliant," he rattled loudly, actually moving across the room to steer the reluctant butler out into the hall. "Now toddle off, good man, toddle off." Reaching forward, Lord Bidwell firmly shut the door in the butler's face, turning to beam in a pleased fashion at the furious Cassie. "Wonderful chap."

"Really, Lord Bidwell," Cassie retorted between clenched teeth, "this is most awkward —"

"I would adore to stay and chat, but I fear

that I must see to my mount. He appeared to have the slightest limp just as we arrived. Quite distressing, I must say. I shall have Tatt's head on a platter if he sold me a nag. *A bientôt,* my lady."

With the briefest bow, the unpredictable man abruptly turned and disappeared through the French windows that had been left open to catch the faint breeze. Thoroughly unhinged by the extraordinary encounter, Cassie reluctantly turned to meet the brilliant blue gaze, refusing to acknowledge the sudden leap of her heart as anything but common annoyance.

This man had no right to burst into her home in such a fashion. And he certainly had no right to be glancing over her diaphanous gown in such a thorough fashion. Deciding that it was time to take matters into her own hands, she determinedly squared her shoulders.

"I presume you have some reason for following me, Lord Mumford?" she demanded in blunt tones, her expression revealing her ill humor at his antics.

He smiled in a slow, utterly unrepentant manner. "First, allow me to apologize for my flamboyant companion. He can be rather . . . persistent when he chooses."

"I would say he can be utterly devious."

"Perhaps, but only with the best of intentions."

"Such as forcing his way into my home?"

The smile only widened. "Come, Lady Greer, Biddles did not precisely force his way into your home. He merely ensured that I was allowed a few moments to speak with you in private."

Oddly disturbed by the knowledge they were indeed alone, Cassie determinedly held on to her icy displeasure.

"I cannot imagine why you would wish to speak with me in private."

He arched a dark brow at her tart remark. "But surely you realized your . . . appearance today in the park was bound to create interest. I assumed you would be delighted by my obvious interest in your charms."

It took a moment for Cassie to fully realize the import of his smooth words; then a painful blush rose to her cheeks. Somehow it had never entered her woolly head that her disguise would lead to such complications. After all, she had never been bothered by unwelcome suitors when she was tramping about her Devonshire estate in shabby gowns and her hair in tangles. And even now she could only wonder if the Irresistible Earl wasn't foxed. Why else would he pursue her when he could have his choice of the most celebrated courtesans?

Whatever the reason, it was clear she would have to do some swift thinking if she were to avoid further difficulties.

"Actually, I went to the park to . . . to meet an acquaintance."

"Acquaintance?"

"Yes."

Folding his arms across his wide chest, Lord Mumford regarded her with uncanny intensity.

"And who is this mysterious acquaintance?"

She wanted to inform him that it was none of his bloody business, but something in the handsome features warned her that this was not a man easily cast aside. She had no doubt aroused his curiosity by her obvious lack of enthusiasm for his exalted presence. After all, a courtesan was dependent on such men to maintain her establishment. It was imperative that she cast aside her shrewish temper and play her role in a more convincing manner if she did not wish the charade to be exposed.

"It would hardly be prudent to discuss my private . . . connections," she retorted, hoping that the late afternoon shadows were hiding her painful embarrassment at uttering the suggestive words.

The blue gaze abruptly narrowed. "You mean to say that your charms are already engaged?"

"I . . . yes."

"What a pity," he murmured, slowly moving forward to regard her heated cheeks with a piercing intensity. "I find you quite intriguing, Lady Greer."

Unnerved by his sudden proximity, Cassie took a swift step backward, nearly tumbling over a hideous lacquer table that matched the rest of the cheap Chinese furnishings.

"I fail to see why, my lord. I am most unremarkable."

"Unremarkable? Come, come, my dear, there is no need for such modesty. You are a beautiful woman. Beautiful enough to expect a companion that will ensure you are properly taken care of." He cast a critical glance around the shabby room, clearly unimpressed by the vulgar décor. "Something your current connection appears incapable of providing."

"I assure you I am quite comfortable."

"But why settle for comfort when I would be quite willing to provide all the luxuries a woman such as yourself desires?"

She eyed him in a wary manner, certain that he must be a bit beetle-headed. What other reason could there be for his annoying persistence?

"I have all the luxuries that I require, my lord. Indeed, there is nothing that you could possible offer me that could sway my affections."

"Really?" An enigmatic smile suddenly curved his full lips. "I admire your loyalty, Lady Greer, but I must warn you that I am not a man who can readily admit defeat. Indeed, there is nothing that I enjoy more than a sporting challenge."

Opening her mouth to inform him that she was not some prize to be won or lost, Cassie was distracted by the entrance of the butler carrying a large tray of tea. Indeed, the tray was so large Cassie could only wonder if the cook had been told that half of London had arrived for tea rather than one slender earl.

"Tea is served, my lady," the butler unnecessarily announced, placing the tray on a low table.

Nearly stamping her foot in frustration, Cassie was forced to meet the amused blue gaze with a semblance of dignified composure. How did one politely offer tea to a gentleman who had just offered her a most improper proposition?

"Would you care for tea, my lord?"

He laughed softly at the stiff words, seeming to find a great deal of amusement in the ridiculous situation.

"As much as I long to stay and further our acquaintance, my lady, I fear I must be off."

Cassie didn't bother to hide her relief. "I see."

"You should, however, warn your secret benefactor."

"Warn?"

"Tell him that I have fallen victim to your persuasive charms," he smoothly murmured, his expression making her heart skip a beat, "and that I will allow nothing to stand in the way of making you mine."

Grasping her hand before she could gauge his intent, Lord Mumford raised her fingers to his warm lips, then outrageously turned over her arm to lightly kiss the tender skin of her delicate wrist. Cassie gasped as an unfamiliar tingle raced through her blood, making her knees decidedly weak and her head spin in a most unnerving fashion. Then, with an elegant bow the raven-haired man was swiftly crossing out of the room and disappearing down the hall.

Absently rubbing her wrist, Cassie listened as the front door closed and the sound of horses clattered down the cobbled street. Really, the man was clearly a scoundrel.

Disdaining eligible young ladies that sought to attract his attention and then ruthlessly pursuing women of easy virtue that he could dismiss at will. She should be taking great pleasure in the knowledge that she was in a position to prove that his wicked charm was far from irresistible. But instead, a shiver of fear raced down her spine.

She had the most unpleasant premonition that Lord Mumford was a danger to more than her charade.

"Well?" Vaulting onto his restless mount, Luke regarded his friend in an expectant manner.

Urging his own horse down the street, Biddles lifted a puzzled brow. "Well, what?"

Swiftly catching up to the brisk pace, Luke heaved an exasperated sigh. "Really, Biddles, I know very well there was nothing wrong with your precious bay. I presume you took the opportunity to find out a bit of information on the tantalizing Lady Greer."

"Perhaps."

"Are you going to tell me, or do I have to put you to the rack?"

"I say, Luke, you are in a bit of a twit over this pampian," Biddles retorted, a speculative gleam in his eye. "Are you quite certain it would not be best to put your oar in less dangerous waters?"

Luke smiled in a wry manner. No doubt his companion was right. He had indeed developed a most uncommon fascination with the alluring Lady Greer. A fascination that had only deepened during the enticing encounter. But while prudence urged him to flee while he was able to do so, he knew quite well he would do no such thing.

"My oar is perfectly fine where it is. Now, did you discover any interesting information or not?"

"Naturally. Have I ever failed you, my most beloved friend?"

"You did leave me waiting in a drafty barn while you delighted yourself with a French countess," Luke reminded his companion in dry tones.

"Are you still digging up that old bone?" Biddles sighed in a mournful manner. "If you will recall, I managed to convince the French countess to smuggle several English prisoners through her estate. Not to mention receiving several cases of fine brandy to warm our cold nights."

"And nearly got us both sent to the guillotine when the count returned home to find you in his bed."

Biddles laughed with obvious enjoyment. "Ah . . . what a fine chase that was. Lucky for us the count never considered searching the convent for two English soldiers."

"Yes, there is nothing quite as delightful as fleeing from a cuckolded husband, but you still have not told me what you have learned."

"Oh, very well, Mumford," Biddles relented. "I happened to pick up several intriguing details from the downstairs maid who was just leaving for the market. She said that Lady Greer rented the house three days ago and arrived with her housekeeper and several gowns recently purchased from a well-known modiste."

"Was that all?"

"No. She also claims that both Lady Greer and her housekeeper appear to have a peculiar interest in finding a woman named Nell."

Luke arched a brow in puzzlement. "Nell?"

"That was all they seemed to know about the woman, except that she used to be on the stage."

"A relative?" Luke pondered aloud. "Or perhaps a friend of the family?"

Biddles shrugged. "I haven't the least notion."

"And what about any callers? Does she have any acquaintances in London?"

"You mean gentlemen acquaintances?"

Luke cast his companion a sour glance. "Yes."

"There are none. Which, of course, is a source of avid curiosity throughout the neighborhood," Biddles retorted. "As a rule, these houses are rented by gentlemen who plan to devote at least a portion of their time with the young ladies within. Lady Greer, however, appears to have mysteriously received an establishment with none of the inconvenience of entertaining her protector."

Ridiculously, Luke experienced a flare of sheer relief. Of course, it was nothing more than gratitude that he hadn't completely lost his ability to judge others, he reassured himself. No man liked to think he could be gulled so easily.

Whatever the reason, he couldn't deny the fierce surge of pleasure to learn that Lady Greer was no common courtesan and that her affections were not nearly so engaged as she had implied.

"So she has no obvious benefactor, and she quite determinedly put paid to my suggestion that I support her in a manner that most women in her position would leap at." Luke narrowed his brilliant eyes to narrow slits. "It would be my deduction that the young woman is not quite what she seems."

As they entered the more reputable part of town, the traffic thickened, and both men were forced to slow their pace to a mere walk. Moving his mount closer, Biddles ensured that they could not be overheard by passing riders.

"Indeed. But what possible reason could a young lady of quality have to risk her reputation in such a daring manner?"

"That is what we have to discover," Luke said, his mind already leaping to the next plan of action. "As well as her connection to this unknown Nell."

Biddles sent him a dry glance. "For once, I fear it will take more than your irresistible charm to convince the young lady to confide her secrets. She appears remarkably stubborn for such a tiny thing."

Stubborn, spirited and quite bewitching, Luke inwardly acknowledged.

"Then we shall have to depend upon our rather dubious talents and find the truth without the aid of Lady Greer," Luke announced.

"And pray, how do you propose to accomplish that?"

"We shall attend the theater, Biddles."

"Pardon me?"

Luke smiled, recalling the sensation of

the fluttering pulse as he had brushed his lips against the velvet smooth skin of her inner wrist.

"You said that all Lady Greer knows of this Nell is her name and the fact she was once on the stage. The next logical step would be to seek information from her former acquaintances. When she arrives, I shall be there waiting."

Four

The crisp morning sunlight did little to improve the dingy theater. Standing on the trash-littered street, Cassie felt her heart sink another notch. This was the fifth theater she had visited in the past three days, each one more disreputable than the last. Clearly, the sudden rush of theaters that had opened in the past few years had not improved the standards of the stage. Indeed, it was clear that most owners were more concerned with greed than art.

Of course, she told herself with a grimace, she had already managed to discern that few of the women who called themselves actresses actually made their livelihood in the theater. Instead, they used their time upon the stage in the hope of attracting a wealthy benefactor. A shocking notion for a gently bred lady. Although, after the past weeks, Cassie was becoming less easily shocked.

After putting aside her natural prejudice, she had discovered that the women she met on the streets each day were not the horrid, grasping doxies she had presumed would inhabit such a location in London, but women like herself, attempting to make

67

their way through the world with no one to depend upon except themselves. That thought had disturbed her more over the past few days than what occurred within their rented homes.

With an effort, Cassie forced her thoughts back to the narrow street. This was no neighborhood in which to be lost in daydreams. Even by London standards, it was dangerous.

Squaring her shoulders, Cassie marched toward the half-opened door, only to jump hastily backward as it was flung open and a servant stomped out to empty a bucket of filthy water onto the street. Cassie discovered herself hesitating at the notion of approaching the stranger. Even with her foolish amount of courage, she felt uneasy.

The man was uncommonly large, with a thick chest and arms usually only seen on a blacksmith. His clothing was rough, and the stale smell of gin overshadowed even the rotting trash. Hardly the sort of man she wished to attract the attention of, but Cassie was becoming desperate. With every passing day, the hopes of retrieving her home and inheritance grew a bit dimmer. Now she forced herself to nervously clear her throat.

"Pardon me."

"Stand aside, luv. Stand aside." The servant never bothered to turn about as he emptied his second bucket.

"But —"

"If yer be looking fer work, we ain't hiring."

"No. I am searching for a . . . friend," Cassie protested, wondering how many poor women would actually seek employment in such an establishment.

"Every lady down here be lookin' fer a friend. I ain't got the quid today. Now move along."

Cassie shuddered. "No. I mean my friend is an actress here. Her name is Nell."

"Nell Maggert?" The dark-haired man abruptly turned about, his bloodshot eyes widening in appreciation at the sight of Cassie. "Well, well, mayhap I do have a quid after all."

Expecting the same suspicious glare and denial that any Nell had been employed at the theater, Cassie forced herself to ignore the leering gaze that drifted over the thick cloak she had possessed the good sense to wear.

Nell Maggert. Could it be the one she was searching for?

"Is Nell here?"

"Naw. She found herself a cove to keep her.

Lit out of here without so much as a farewell."

Cassie felt her heart leap. "You must mean Herbie?"

"That's the bloke. Short, red-headed fella with a nasty temper."

"I need to speak with Nell. Could you give me her new address?"

A furrow of puzzlement drew the heavy brows together. The man might not possess a keen intelligence, but he could obviously detect that her educated voice and expensive clothing were distinctly out of place.

"Yer say yer a friend of Nell's?"

"Yes."

Without warning, the door to the theater was once again shoved open.

"A friend of Nell's?" a second male voice demanded. "Then why didn't yer know where she be?"

Cassie turned to discover a young man with a thin face and narrow blue eyes regarding her with unnerving intensity. Oddly, there was something in his sharp features that made her even more uneasy than his brutish companion did.

"I . . . have been out of town," she swiftly lied.

"I think yer be lying."

"Mind yer tongue, Toby," the large man growled.

70

A humorless smile twisted Toby's thin lips. "Seems a mite peculiar to me. She don't look like any friend of Nell's."

"Perhaps not, but she can be a friend of mine," the large man argued, dropping his buckets to slowly move toward Cassie. "What do yer say?"

Barely preventing herself from bolting in panic, Cassie backed away.

"Unfortunately, I have to be leaving. My groom has a carriage waiting for me around the corner."

The desperate lie halted the older man, but Toby was clearly more astute. His smile widened as he noted her trembling lips.

"You can't be leaving so soon. Not before you tell us your interest in Nell."

"Perhaps I can return tomorrow," Cassie managed to stammer, her heart slamming against her chest as the thin man suddenly lunged to catch her arm in a violent grip.

"I want to be knowin' today," he insisted, his expression chilling Cassie to the bone.

Quite certain that a scream in this neighborhood would be a useless waste of breath, Cassie prepared to defend herself as fiercely as she could. She couldn't possibly win, but she was not about to concede defeat without a fight.

Lifting her foot to provide a sharp kick to

the scoundrel's knee, she was abruptly halted by the sound of a familiar voice that nearly made her faint in relief.

"Troubles, Lady Greer?" Luke drawled from behind.

"Lord Mumford," she breathed as the fox-faced man reluctantly loosened his grip and backed away. She didn't even protest when the vexing lord stepped next to her and wrapped an intimate arm about her shoulders. Her only feeling was overwhelming happiness that she had been rescued from her own stupidity.

"Are you acquainted with these gentlemen?" he inquired in dangerously soft tones.

The larger man gave an awkward bow even as his evil leer was replaced with a grating smile.

"My lord, such an honor. A real honor, it be."

With a graceful motion, Lord Mumford lifted his quizzing glance to peer at the two men.

"I presume that you have work to attend to?"

"Oh . . . yes, yes indeed." The large servant bowed again, reaching out to cuff his obviously less impressed companion with his ham-shaped fist. "Come along, Toby."

Just for a moment the thin-faced man continued to glare at Cassie; then with a small shrug he slowly turned to follow his partner. As the door to the theater closed, Cassie released a shaky breath.

She had been saved. Even if it was by the gentleman that only the previous evening she had declared the last man in London she wished to encounter. Lifting her head, she formed the reluctant words to thank him. But, predictably, she didn't manage to utter a word before he was smiling in mocking amusement.

"What a delightful surprise, Lady Greer," he drawled. "I had no notion you were a theater lover."

Her warm flare of gratitude died a swift death, to be replaced by her more familiar suspicion. What the devil was this man doing here? It was decidedly unlikely for him to have chosen this particular street on this particular morning to travel.

Unless, of course, he had once again followed her.

Why the blazes could he not leave her be? she wondered with a flare of annoyance. As relieved as she might be at his timely arrival, she remained thoroughly aware that he posed a danger of his own. Pulling away from his lingering gasp, she regarded him with a narrowed gaze.

"Nor I you, sir," she retorted in tart tones.

"It appears that we have a vast deal in common. A favorable sign, I think," he said smoothly, then held out his arm. "But come, let us leave this distasteful place. I will drive you home."

Her chin instinctively tilted. His request was far too close to a command.

"Thank you, but that is not necessary."

His expression became one of long suffering. "Lady Greer, you have already discovered just how dangerous this neighborhood can be to a woman on her own. Unless you enjoy the attentions of such men?"

"Do not be absurd."

He held out an arm. "Then, shall we go?"

Ridiculously, Cassie hesitated. She had no desire to spend more time with Lord Mumford. Not when they would be virtually alone in the closed carriage she had spotted waiting down the street. Then sanity at last prevailed.

She had been a thorough ninny to come down to this place alone. She would be even more of a ninny to remain.

Still, she could muster little grace as she conceded defeat.

"Very well."

With a smile, Luke took her arm and led her to the glossy black carriage. Waving aside the uniformed groom, he carefully lifted her into the shadowed interior. Anxious to rid herself of his disturbing touch, Cassie hastily scrambled to a padded corner. Of course, the vexing man planted himself shockingly close to her side. He did not even pretend it was accidental that his hard body was pressed next to her own.

A tiny shiver wracked her form as the heat and scent of him surrounded her. For goodness sakes, she thought in exasperation, what right did this gentleman have to unsettle her in such a manner? It was positively disgraceful.

Seemingly unaffected by the same tingle of excitement that raced through her own blood, Luke stretched out his Hessian-clad legs and tugged down his dove gray coat.

"I must say, my opinion of your benefactor is becoming increasingly low," he murmured as the carriage rolled down the cobbled street. "What sort of gentleman allows a woman to endanger herself by frequenting such a disreputable place?"

With an effort, Cassie gathered her scattered wits. She could not afford to be distracted. Not when this man could easily destroy her reputation.

"He does not dictate where I may or may not go," she said in stiff tones.

"Ah, a woman of spirit."

She unwisely turned to meet his glittering gaze. "I suppose you prefer those women who are properly demure and always bow to the superior whims of gentlemen?"

His gaze deliberately lowered to the fullness of her mouth. "I thought I had made it very clear that what I prefer is . . . you, Lady Greer."

Cassie felt her face flame at the suggestive hint of huskiness in his tone.

"I wish you would stop saying such things."

"Very well." He smiled with wicked amusement, his gaze trailing over her pale features framed by the cloud of red hair. "I will instead say that you appear remarkably charming this morning. Even swathed from head to toe like the most prim of spinsters you manage to provoke a man's passion. I wish to brush aside that cloak and discover what delights lie beneath."

"Lord Mumford, that is enough," Cassie snapped in outraged tones. Really, the man was beyond the pale. It was bad enough that they were alone in the carriage and that he was practically seated in her lap. To speak in such intimate terms was positively decadent. Her temper was not soothed by his sudden chuckle. "What do you find so amusing, sir?"

"You, my lady."

"I fail to see why," she retorted icily.

Shifting to gain a better view of her flushed countenance, Luke tilted his head to one side.

"You dress and attempt to act like a courtesan, but you blush like a schoolgirl with every compliment."

"That is ridiculous."

A raven brow arched. "Even more intriguing is the fact you are obviously determined to rebuff my very generous advances."

"I have told you . . . my affections are engaged."

"Ah yes, the elusive gentleman who has first claim on your emotions," he mocked.

Her blush deepened. "Precisely."

"Really, Lady Greer, you do not strike me as a fool." He regarded her in shrewd disbelief. "A woman in your position does not lightly toss aside a business proposition that might very well secure your future for years to come. Particularly when your current situation leaves much to be desired."

Cassie swallowed a nervous lump. His accusation defied any rational argument. He was perfectly correct. A woman in her supposed position would not dismiss his attentions. She would, in fact, do whatever necessary to secure his promise of a greater financial reward.

Still, she could hardly admit that she had no need of his generous offer. She could only hope that he tired of this ridiculous game before he discovered the truth.

"I am quite comfortable in my current position," she lamely protested, unsurprised when he rewarded her lie with a scathing glance.

"You are comfortable with a man who leaves you in a tawdry home with less than a handful of servants and proceeds to treat you with such obvious indifference?" he demanded.

"It is really none of your concern."

"I should never treat you in such a shabby fashion."

Cassie once again experienced that delicious shiver. She had no doubt that this man would be a most passionate lover. There was an undeniable hint of sensuality in the generous curve of his mouth and the possessiveness in his manner. He would never be casual in his relationships. He would demand and give total devotion.

With a sense of relief, she felt the carriage slow to a halt. She needed to be away from

Lord Mumford and his disturbing presence to clear her rattled wits.

"Thank you for bringing me home, my lord," she muttered, not bothering to wait for the groom as she shoved the carriage door open.

In an awkward motion she crawled through the door and onto the street. Turning about, she gave a small jump as she realized Luke had followed her.

"Am I not to be invited in for tea?" he drawled.

She had no doubt he was attempting to taunt her, and she barely resisted the urge to box his ears.

"I fear I am occupied this morning."

"How unfortunate." He gave a mocking bow. "Then I suppose I shall have to call later in the day."

"I . . ." Meeting the glittering blue gaze, Cassie realized that arguments would be futile. Instead, she resolved to make very clear to her butler that she was not receiving visitors. Especially visitors by the name of Lord Mumford and Lord Bidwell. "Good day, my lord."

Hoping she appeared more dignified than she felt, Cassie swept up the narrow walk and through the door that was hastily pulled open by a footman.

All in all, it had proven to be yet another disastrous day in London.

Watching Cassie regally stalk away, Luke allowed a smile of pleasure to curve his mouth.

What a delightful creature, he silently mused. Spirited, beautiful and with a hint of mystery that he found irresistible.

With every meeting, he discovered himself more and more determined to unravel the web of secrecy she wrapped about herself. To discover the truth of Lady Greer.

He would stake his life that she was no common courtesan.

Then his smile was suddenly replaced by a frown.

For the past three mornings he had followed her through the streets of London at a discreet distance. He had carefully watched her enter one theater after another. But this morning his heart had nearly stopped at the sight of the two ruffians attempting to manhandle her.

What if he hadn't been there? What if he had overslept? Or decided she wasn't worth the bother?

Even now she could be lying on that filthy street. Or worse, in that hovel of a theater at the mercy of those brutes.

It did not bear thinking of.

A strange, wholly unexpected flare of frustration rushed through his heart. It was ludicrous. This woman was a complete stranger. She could not even claim a passing acquaintanceship, but he couldn't deny an overwhelming urge to protect her from her own foolishness.

She shouldn't be in this house, and certainly not in this neighborhood, he thought with an unexplainable obstinacy. And she most certainly should not be trailing through streets even the Watch avoided. But she was clearly determined to risk her lovely neck, and he could do nothing to halt her absurd behavior. Not without locking her in his wine cellar, which was a surprisingly tempting thought.

Just as vexing was the knowledge he could not possibly be constantly on hand to sweep her out of danger.

He would simply have to uncover the truth. Perhaps then he would know how to bring the stubborn chit to her senses.

Luke turned back toward the carriage, intending to seek his long overdue breakfast. But as he stepped forward, a slight movement at the far side of the hedge captured his attention.

"What the devil?"

Not even hesitating Luke darted up the path next to the house, cautiously edging his way to the corner. With the same caution, he peered around the edge, his body stiffening in surprise at the sight of the thin, ragged man sticking his head through an open widow. It was apparent even from a distance that he was up to no good. What sort of man peered through a lady's window?

Luke shifted his weight as he prepared to leap forward and catch the lurker, but a stray branch snapped beneath his boots, alerting the stranger to his presence.

With a gasp, the man turned around, the thin face twisting into a furious scowl as he realized he had been spotted.

A surge of disbelief raced through Luke as he recognized the narrow features and murderous eyes. *Damn.* The man from the theater. He had obviously followed them as they had crawled through the tedious London traffic, and now he knew precisely where to find Lady Greer.

Luke charged forward, determined to capture the scoundrel and force him to confess his interest in Lady Greer, but he underestimated the wily man's speed. With a muffled curse, the stranger bolted toward the back of the house, using his small size to easily slip through a hole in the hedge. Luke skidded to a halt, in enough possession of his faculties to realize that his broad frame would never squeeze through such a tiny space. It was equally obvious that he would never have time to round the hedge and catch the blackguard. The rat would have swiftly vanished among the mews by now.

Luke clenched his fists in frustration. What the blazes was happening? There was more intrigue stirring about this establishment than in all of Europe. And without knowing what bubblebath the mysterious Lady Greer had tumbled into, he had no means of protecting her.

"May I help you, my lord?"

Turning toward the house, Luke saw the granite-faced butler standing in the tradesman door. A sudden notion flickered through his mind.

"I was searching for the man I spotted peering into Lady Greer's window."

"A man, my lord?"

"A short man with a dark gray coat."

"How very peculiar."

"Peculiar indeed." Luke reached into his coat to withdraw a small embossed card. "This is my address. If this . . . gentleman or any other gentleman returns, I wish to know as soon as possible."

"Of course."

Luke again reached into his coat, this time to withdraw several pound notes.

"And I would appreciate having someone within the household keeping a close guard on Lady Greer. She possesses the most absurd belief that she is impervious to danger."

With swift efficiency the butler pocketed the offered money and performed a stiff bow.

"I understand completely, my lord. You can depend upon me."

"Thank you."

Luke was not precisely reassured as he strode back to the carriage. The butler had accepted his bribe far too readily and was clearly for hire to the highest bidder. Luke's only hope was that whoever wished to harm Lady Greer did not possess his own vast resources.

Absently allowing his groom to help him into the carriage, Luke gave the order to head for Lord Bidwell's home. His breakfast was momentarily forgotten. This was decidedly a muddle that could use the unique skills of the devious little man, he decided.

Settling back in the leather squabs, Luke

brooded on the tangle as he traveled through the city toward the more respectable streets of London. He barely noted the cries of the vendors or shouts from the drivers as they attempted to negotiate the crowded streets. Instead, he attempted to rationally consider the situation and how best to approach a solution.

After a considerable drive, they at last pulled to a halt in front of Biddle's lavish establishment. Luke hurriedly descended from the carriage and swept his way up the long steps. Not surprisingly, the butler favored him with a curious glance as he opened the door and led him into the wide foyer.

"I fear His Lordship is not yet down this morning," he apologized as he accepted Luke's coat and hat.

"Never fear, Thomas, I shall beard the lion in his den. Would you have breakfast sent up? Eggs and kidneys would do nicely. Oh, and a pot of coffee. I have a feeling we shall need it."

"Very good, my lord."

Accustomed to Luke's familiar manner within the household, the butler merely bowed and retreated toward the back of the town house.

Taking the steps two at a time, Luke

moved down the hall to Biddles's private dressing room. He shoved open the door without so much as a knock to discover the rat-faced man seated on a padded chair as his valet carefully knotted his cravat.

"Good God, Luke," Lord Bidwell drawled in mild reproach. "Do you know the time?"

"I have need of your talents," Luke announced without preamble, lowering his large form onto a delicate chaise longue.

"I have been telling you that for years, old chap." Biddles carefully turned to run a critical gaze over Luke's elegant coat. "Only a gentleman in his dotage would choose such a drab attire. I shall ensure that by the end of the month you acquire the most talked of wardrobe in London."

Luke gave a visible shudder. "I was not referring to your ghastly preference in fashion, thank goodness. I wish for you to make a few discreet inquiries."

"Ah, how dreary." Lifting a thin hand, Biddles waved aside the hovering valet. "That will be all, Emerson."

"Very well, my lord."

With a small bow, the silver-haired man who had been at Biddles's side since he left Oxford silently withdrew from the chamber. Biddles leaned forward to peer in the oval mirror. With a grimace, he reached up to give a few expert tugs on the starched linen.

"A pity I cannot discover a valet who can be discreet as well as tie a decent cravat. As it is, I must suffer this sadly predictable knot for the promise of privacy." Biddles gave another tug; then, reluctantly satisfied, he leaned back to regard Luke with a shrewd gaze. "Now, what inquiries do you require?"

"I wish you to discover the whereabouts of an actress named Nell Maggert. She might be connected with a gentleman who goes by the endearment of Herbie."

"Egad, still dangling after Lady Greer, are we?"

"I am not . . . dangling."

"Certainly not," Biddles mocked. "You always trail after unknown women, force your way into their homes and then waste both of our time seeking actresses named Nell."

Luke allowed the merest smile to curve his lips. "Perhaps I am dangling a bit."

"A very dangerous habit, old boy. Still, you are clearly determined to behave like the veriest moonling over this chit."

Luke refused to rise to the bait. For now, his concern for Lady Greer's safety was too great to ponder his own odd behavior.

"Will you help me, Biddles?"

There was a pause; then Biddles gave a shrug of defeat. "But of course. Where shall we begin? With Herbie? A man of society or a cit?"

A rush of relief eased the tension in Luke's body. He possessed full confidence in this man's abilities. Locating a mere actress and her benefactor should prove little challenge to his skills.

"Difficult to say," he responded. "Wealthy enough at least to maintain a separate household for his mistress."

"La. Prinny maintains any number of households without a farthing to his name."

"I doubt that Herbie possesses such royal privilege," Luke pointed out in dry tones.

"Perhaps not." Biddles narrowed his gaze. "Tell me, Luke, what do you intend to do while I am gadding about London in search of this mysterious Nell?"

A glint of anticipation flickered to life in the depths of the deep blue eyes.

"I shall be enjoying tea with the lovely Lady Greer."

"Indeed?" Biddles arched a brow. "Were you invited?"

"Let us say that I invited myself."

Biddles favored him with a long, considering survey before slowly leaning forward.

"You do realize that this seeming reluctance might very well be a cunning lure?"

"A lure?"

"How better to catch the attention of the Irresistible Earl than by pretending complete indifference?" he demanded. "There are few things more enticing than attaining the unattainable."

Luke could not deny the truth in his friend's warning. It had occurred to him on more than one occasion that Lady Greer's seeming reluctance might be an elaborate ploy. Even the impression that she was in some mysterious peril might be a hoax.

Still, he found himself shying from the unpleasant thought. No woman could conjure the innocence he had detected in the depths of her silver eyes. No matter how great an actress.

"Not all of us possess your devious nature, Biddles," he protested in a light tone.

Biddles smiled in a cynical fashion. "Most gentlemen and all ladies possess devious natures, my friend. Do not allow yourself to be led on a fool's journey. It might cost you more than a few quid."

Luke swallowed his instinctive protest. His friend was reading far too much into his interest in Lady Greer. Certainly he was concerned for her safety. And perhaps he was somewhat fascinated by her elusive charms. But to imply that he was in danger of losing his heart. Why, it was ludicrous. Absurd.

"You have no need to worry on my account, Biddles," he promised. Then oddly discomfited by the course of the conversation, he glanced toward the door. "My only danger at the moment is to my sadly neglected stomach. Where the devil is my breakfast?"

"This is the place, my lord." Jameson pointed at the narrow brick building. "She came out and stepped right in me path. Nearly stopped me heart, it did."

"Thank you, Jameson."

Luke stepped out of the carriage and regarded the less than impressive office with a narrowed gaze. It had been nearly a week since he had rescued the impetuous Lady Greer from her absurd visit to the theater district. A week that he had devoted to uncovering the truth behind the maiden's mysterious charade, only to fail in the most dismal fashion.

Much to his chagrin, Lady Greer remained thoroughly impervious to his supposedly irresistible charms. His daily visits were greeted with an icy displeasure, and his subtle attempts to unmask her secrets were cut decidedly short. It was quite obvious that he had at last met his match.

Eventually, desperation had forced him to seek his answers in another direction. His first meeting with Lady Greer had been in front of this building. Her reason for being there had to give some clue to her transformation from a country Miss to an elegant courtesan.

A few discreet inquiries had revealed that a Mr. Albert Carson currently rented the building, and that he would eagerly oblige Lord Mumford with a meeting at his convenience. They also revealed Mr. Carson to be a staunch, rather humorless gentleman who was quite above bribery and never gossiped about his clients. His one weakness was an ambition to attract a family of quality to represent.

Luke fully intended to use such an ambition to his advantage.

"I shall be a few moments, Jameson."

"Very good, my lord." Jameson gave a slight bow before leaping back onto the carriage.

Luke crossed to the door and entered the narrow hall. His Hessians echoed through the stiff silence as he made his way to the office. At his entrance, a thin, nearly bald-headed gentleman jumped to his feet.

"My lord, please come in. This is indeed a pleasure," he stammered, pulling forward a refurbished chair. "Would you care for tea? Or perhaps you prefer brandy?"

Luke waved a negligent hand as he strolled to lower his large frame in the seat.

"Nothing for me, thank you."

"Very well." Mr. Carson gave a reluctant nod as he resumed his place behind the ancient desk. "Now, how may I be of service, my lord?"

Luke carefully maintained an air of negligent boredom. He did not wish to create any suspicion about his interest in the golden-haired maiden. Stretching out his legs, he gave a faint shrug.

"Actually, I have a rather peculiar request."

"Oh?"

"A fortnight ago, I encountered a young lady leaving your establishment. She possessed golden hair and was attired in a gray gown."

The Man of Business gave a startled cough. Whatever he had been expecting from Luke, it was certainly not this.

"Is there any particular reason for your interest?" he cautiously hedged.

Luke suppressed a wry grin, wondering if the man thought him to be a debaucher of young, innocent ladies.

"She dropped a pair of gloves. I wish to return them."

Mr. Carson appeared far from appeased by the glib lie.

"How very kind," he murmured. "But there is no need for you to be bothered with such a trivial matter. If you give me the gloves, I will gladly see that they are returned."

"I prefer to return them myself." Luke's tone defied argument.

"Oh, but —"

"I, of course, require her name and address."

"My lord." The man ran a nervous hand over his head, clearly torn between loyalty to his client and a desire to please his illustrious visitor. "I fear that is impossible."

"Nonsense. Nothing is impossible."

"I cannot possibly give out the young lady's name."

"Why?"

Mr. Carson gave an uncomfortable smile. "It is a matter of discretion. You understand, my lord."

"Frankly, I do not," Luke drawled. "I merely wish to return a pair of gloves."

The gentleman cleared his throat, obviously wishing that he could crawl beneath his desk.

"A young lady cannot be overly cautious in such times," he attempted to soothe.

Luke arched an imperious brow, using his commanding presence to his full advantage.

"Surely, Mr. Carson, you are not implying that my intentions toward this young lady are of an unsavory nature?"

The poor man gave a strangled noise, his eyes protruding in sudden anxiety.

"No, certainly not. I . . . That is . . ."

"Yes?"

Mr. Carson squirmed beneath Luke's piercing regard, the battle between his stiff morals and his worldly ambitions waging beneath the surface. At last his ambition overcame his pesky principles, and he gave a shaky laugh.

"Yes, well, perhaps there would be no harm."

Luke smiled in satisfaction. There were times when his vast inheritance came in decidedly handy.

"Certainly not."

"The young lady is Miss Cassandra Stanholte. I believe she prefers to go by Cassie."

"Cassie," Luke breathed, feeling a fierce stab of relief. At last a name for his mysterious maiden.

"From Devonshire," Mr. Carson completed.

"Do you have her address in London?"

"She has no residence in London. Indeed, her visit was quite brief. She has already returned to her estate."

Luke was not surprised the Man of Business was unaware that Miss Stanholte was far closer than Devonshire. She had gone to great lengths to disguise her presence in London.

The question was, why?

"What a pity." He pretended an absorbed interest in the cuff of his deep jade green coat. "I presume she resides with her parents?"

"Her parents unfortunately died in an accident several years ago."

"Then she possesses a guardian?"

"It is a rather . . . unconventional household, my lord," Mr. Carson conceded, his grimace revealing his disapproval of the situation. "Miss Stanholte is a very independent young lady and not easily persuaded she has need of a guardian."

Luke swallowed a chuckle. He was wretchedly familiar with Miss Stanholte's independent nature. And not remotely shocked that she would refuse the protection of a guardian.

At least he now understood how she managed to disappear into the disreputable neighborhood without creating a scandal. There was no one to wonder what had become of Miss Stanholte or to question why she had not returned from London.

"Indeed. She at least depends upon you

for her business advice." He favored the gentleman with a slight smile. "I presume that was her reason for traveling to London?"

A pained expression of regret tightened the thin face. "I really must insist that my business with Miss Stanholte remain in confidence, my lord."

Luke subdued his instinctive desire to demand that the Man of Business reveal the truth of Miss Stanholte's visit to London. How else could he discover the reason for her bizarre behavior? But the realization that such a demand would only confirm that his interest in the maiden was far from casual held his tongue.

"Ah, well, I will ensure that my secretary has the gloves delivered to Miss Stanholte in Devonshire."

Mr. Carson smiled in relief. "I am certain she will be most appreciative. Although I would prefer that you not mention my name."

"Certainly not." With a languid grace, Luke rose to his feet. It appeared he had pressed the man as far as he dared. At least for the moment. "Thank you, Mr. Carson."

Leaping to his feet, Mr. Carson gave a nervous bow.

"Please let me know if I can be of further service, my lord."

"Yes, I will."

With a faint nod, Luke turned to leave the small office.

Miss Cassandra Stanholte of Devonshire.

He turned the name over and over in his mind as he moved down the hall and into the street. At his appearance, the glossy carriage pulled forward and the groom leapt down to open the door.

"To Lady Greer's," he commanded as he climbed into the leather seat.

Settling himself comfortably, Luke allowed a smile of anticipation to curve his lips.

Several streets away, Cassie forced herself to calmly sit on the sofa and enjoy her tea. Or at least to pretend to enjoy her tea. Not for the world would she admit that she was anxiously dreading the arrival of the annoying Lord Mumford.

The man was a wretched nuisance, she told herself sternly. Every day he appeared without warning, as if he possessed the right to treat her home with such casual intimacy. No matter how often she repulsed his advances or threatened to have him thrown from her house, he simply refused to leave her in peace. And while a more vain female might accept his flirtatious banter at face value, Cassie had not missed the piercing questions and the occasional frown of suspicion she caught on his handsome countenance.

For reasons best known to himself, Lord Mumford had developed an absurd interest in her arrival in this neighborhood, and for the life of her, Cassie could not conceive how to dismiss his attentions.

Even worse, she could not convince her staff that the annoying man was not a welcome visitor to her home.

It was little wonder she was as susceptible to her nerves as any vaporish Miss.

With an abrupt motion, she tossed aside the untasted sponge cake. This was ridiculous. She had far more serious matters to dwell upon than the Irresistible Earl and his peculiar ability to ruffle her staunch composure. Besides which, today she had set her housekeeper to watch the door. Lord Mumford might be able to charm his way past the London servants, but he would find himself hard-pressed to outmaneuver the implacable Mary Green.

Determined to bend her thoughts upon her more pressing troubles, Cassie suddenly froze as a shadow fell across the open

French doors. This was not the first shadow that had caught her attention. Although she could never confirm her suspicion, Cassie had more than once possessed the sensation she was being spied upon. Now that familiar tingle of apprehension inched down her spine, and she slowly rose to her feet.

Was there someone skulking outside her house? Someone who suspected there was more to her presence than just another fallen woman? Or, more frightening, someone who hoped to take advantage of a young lady without the protection of her family?

On the point of calling for help, Cassie watched as the shadow abruptly disappeared, only to be replaced by a large, all too familiar form. In an instant, her fear faded to anger as she watched Lord Mumford casually stride through the open door and into the salon.

Her eyes narrowed in exasperation. Obviously, having been turned aside by Mrs. Green, he had simply rounded the house and waltzed in as if he had every right to come and go as he pleased.

Did the gentleman not comprehend the word *no?*

Unhinged as much by her initial flare of fear as by Lord Mumford's outrageous arrogance, Cassie favored him with a forbidding frown.

"Really, sir, you are —"

"Maddening? Vexing? Irresistibly charming?" he interrupted with a wicked smile.

"Bloody impossible," Cassie muttered to herself, attempting to ignore the treacherous flutter of her heart. Not an easy task, considering the gentleman offered a most captivating sight in his jade coat and tan pantaloons.

How was she to concentrate when her gaze longed to linger on the noble lines of his countenance and the inviting shimmer in his blue eyes?

With an effort, she subdued her unruly thoughts. Tilting her chin, she eyed him squarely.

"Surely, my lord, there must be some house in all of London where your presence is actually welcome?"

"Countless." His smile only widened as he moved farther into the room. "I will have you know that my visits are in the greatest demand. Indeed, I have been assured by more than one hostess that my mere presence is enough to ensure the success of her gathering."

"Poppycock," Cassie muttered before she could halt the word.

Surprisingly, Lord Mumford tilted back his head to chuckle in rich amusement.

"Rather my sentiments as well."

She regarded him in disbelief, "Really?"

"I have little patience with such drivel. I assure you my company was not so avidly sought when I was another penniless earl." He lifted a quizzing glass to survey a lacquer chair with its red satin cushions. "Egad, what a repulsive object. I presume that it is safe to sit upon?"

"I do not recall inviting you to sit."

"No doubt because you did not." He dropped the quizzing glass to regard her with that insufferable amusement. "However, I am gracious enough to ignore your questionable manners."

Her hands clenched in frustration. "Now see here, my lord —"

"Yes, yes, my dear," he drawled. "You are about to demand that I leave. I will refuse. You will then make a number of threats, which I will ignore. In the end I will still be here and you will have caused yourself a great deal of unnecessary aggravation. Why do you not simply concede defeat and ring for tea?"

Cassie stamped her foot. He had to be the most infuriating gentleman in all of England.

"If I were not a woman on my own, you would not be taking advantage of me in this infamous manner."

He lifted his dark brows. "I hardly consider requesting tea taking advantage of you."

"A true gentleman would respect my wishes."

Surprisingly, his smile faded to be replaced by that narrowed gaze that always made her fear he could see straight to her heart.

"You are quite fortunate that I am indeed a gentleman."

She stiffened. "Pardon me?"

With slow, deliberate steps he moved forward to stand directly in front of her.

"As you have just pointed out, you are a woman on your own. That unfortunately leaves you at the mercy of a vast array of men, many of whom would demand more than tea from you."

Cassie could not prevent the heat from crawling beneath her skin. His words struck too close to her earlier unease.

"You are the only gentleman who bothers me, my lord," she weakly countered.

"Good God, are you being deliberately obtuse?" he demanded. "I would think even someone of your stubborn nature would accept the danger of being in such a neighborhood."

"This is none of your concern."

"What if I had been some gentleman who presumed he possessed the right to demand your attentions? Or a ruffian like those you encountered at the theater?"

Her color receded to leave her pale, but she refused to admit the truth of his words. How could she?

"I have no desire to discuss this with you."

"Because you know you are being a fool."

"I am quite capable of taking care of myself. I do not need your assistance."

The blue eyes darkened at her angry challenge; then, without warning, he reached up to grasp her chin with slender fingers.

"Of all the ridiculous things you have said, I believe that is the most absurd."

His touch sent a sharp tingle of awareness down her spine, and Cassie felt her breath catch in her throat. He was so close. She could feel the heat of his body and smell the hint of sandalwood that clung to his warm skin.

"Why will you not leave me in peace?" she pleaded softly.

The unnerving gaze lowered to study the tremble of her soft lips.

"Perhaps I wish to teach you a valuable lesson," he murmured.

"I have no desire to learn any lessons from you, sir."

He ignored her unsteady words, his hand moving to softly brush her cheek. Cassie shivered at the rash of sensations that flared to life.

"Such beautiful skin. Softer than the most expensive silk."

Cassie struggled to breathe as her heart pounded out of control.

"Please . . ."

"And eyes the color of a dove."

"Stop this."

The dark head bent even closer, and Cassie felt her body tremble in delicious anticipation.

" 'Never have I laid eyes on equal beauty in man or woman. I am hushed indeed.' You tempt a man beyond all reason, Lady Greer," he whispered in husky tones.

"My lord." Cassie barely recognized her own voice. "I must insist that you leave."

"But why?" The disturbing fingers trailed the length of her jaw, then halted on the frantic pulse beating in her neck. "Is this not why you dress in such a provocative manner? Why you live in this neighborhood and parade yourself in the park? You wish to attract the attentions of a rich gentleman. Well, you have succeeded. I am very, very attracted."

Cassie gave a slow shake of her head. She should be furious. Outraged at his audacious behavior. No matter what he might think of her position, she was a lady who deserved his respect. Even if he was merely attempting to teach her a lesson.

But rather than fury, it was a treacherous heat that flowed through her blood.

"No . . . I mean . . ."

"Yes? What do you mean?" His breath brushed her flushed cheek. "That you wish me to do this?" His mouth lowered to claim her lips in a soft, searching kiss. Cassie moaned as the disturbing lips caressed and teased, then moved to press against the lids of her eyes that had strangely slid shut. "And this?" he breathed, nuzzling his way down to the sensitive line of her neck.

"No." With an effort, Cassie attempted to clear her foggy thoughts. Her body quivered as his mouth searched ever lower. "If you do not leave, I will scream."

Laughing softly, Luke lifted his head to regard her with smoldering eyes.

"It will do little good. The staff is paid to leave us strictly alone when I am visiting."

It took a moment for his words to sink

through the thick fog in her mind; then her eyes widened with disbelief.

The arrogance of this man.

"How dare you?"

"Very easily," he retorted without apology.

She moved to sweep past him, only to be abruptly halted as his arm encircled her waist and he tugged her against the hard contours of his form. A shudder of delight coursed through her body before she was sternly subduing her unruly reaction to his touch.

"Unhand me, sir."

He smiled at her breathless tone. "For a lady so capable of fending for herself, you are finding it remarkably difficult to rid yourself of one mere gentleman."

"This is not amusing, Lord Mumford," she gritted.

"It is not meant to be, Lady Greer," he countered. "I wish you to realize just how vulnerable you are in this house."

She had never been more poignantly aware of her vulnerability, she acknowledged.

Every nerve tingled with life, and her mouth still carried the branding heat of his lips. A most unnerving condition for a woman who had never before been kissed.

"Please, my lord, no more lessons," she muttered.

Something seemed to flicker deep in the blue eyes, but his expression remained unrelenting.

"Then you agree you cannot remain here?"

"I agree to nothing."

He heaved an exasperated sigh. "Have the past few moments taught you nothing, then?"

Cassie was uncertain whether she wanted to probe into what she might have learned in the past few moments. It was enough to acknowledge that this gentleman could disturb her in a manner that was beyond her control.

"It has taught me that you are a disgraceful cad, Lord Mumford."

"Why, you aggravating minx." He shook his head, even as a reluctant smile tugged at his lips. "Are you always this reluctant to accept reasonable advice, or is it simply because the advice comes from me?"

"I have no need of advice, especially from you —"

Her angry words were interrupted as the door to the salon was thrust open to reveal an impassive Tolson.

"Pardon me, my lady," he intoned, not

seeming to notice that Cassie was currently pressed to Lord Mumford in a most intimate fashion. "But you have a visitor."

Deeply embarrassed to have been caught in such a compromising position, Cassie hastily scrambled away from Luke's lingering grasp and nervously pressed a hand to her heart.

"A visitor?"

"Yes. A rather disreputable young lady. I attempted to send her on her way, but —"

"Tell her it be about Nell," a nasal female voice shrilled from the hall. "I ain't here to beg."

Cassie's emotional turmoil was momentarily forgotten as she felt a sudden flare of excitement. After an entire week of vainly attempting to conjure a means of continuing her search for the elusive Nell, it appeared the answer might have marched onto her very doorstep.

"Send her in, Tolson. And please bring in tea."

Raising a hand to smooth her ruffled curls, Cassie missed the butler's swift glance toward Lord Mumford, and the elegant gentleman's subtle nod.

"Very well." Tolson gave a precise bow before backing out of the room.

With a sharp motion, Cassie turned to

meet the bland regard of her unwelcome intruder. She had no time for polite tactics, she decided as she unconsciously squared her shoulders.

"I must beg you to leave, my lord."

Predictably, he folded his arms across the broad width of his chest.

"I prefer to remain."

"No," she retorted bluntly. She had to rid herself of this tenacious man. "This is a private matter."

"Private or not, I am not about to leave you with some strange woman from the streets. For all you know, she might have some companion waiting in the bushes for an opportunity to slip inside while you are distracted."

She shook her head in exasperated disbelief. Of all the women in London, why the devil had he chosen her to bother?

"It is none of your concern."

He rolled his eyes heavenward. "Not that tedious argument again, Lady Greer? I am not leaving, and that is the end of the matter."

Cassie gritted her teeth, wondering if she possessed the nerve to call for the Watch. It might be amusing to see the elegant lord hauled away as a public nuisance. But the knowledge that she would never dare call such attention to herself halted the brief fantasy.

Instead, she bestowed him with a glare that would have flayed a lesser man.

"Some day, Lord Mumford, I will make you rue your interference."

He smiled as he offered her a mocking bow. "I await that day with great anticipation. Until then, shall we see what our guest has to say?"

Six

The entrance of a short, round-faced girl with frizzed brown hair and ill-fitted gown forced Cassie to curb her irritation with Lord Mumford. There would no doubt be ample time later to be annoyed with the interfering gentleman.

With an effort, she summoned a welcoming smile. "Please come in, Miss . . . ?"

"Stone. Millie Stone," the girl reluctantly supplied, her pale blue gaze nervously darting around the room. Her eyes widened in alarm at the sight of the forbiddingly large gentleman leaning with nonchalant ease against the mantel.

With a sour glare at her uninvited guest, Cassie made the grudging introduction.

"Lord Mumford, may I introduce Miss Stone?"

Luke offered a faint nod of his dark head. "Miss Stone."

"And I am Lady Greer." Cassie attempted to distract the anxious Millie from Luke's cool appraisal. The poor girl appeared as if she might bolt at any moment.

"Yes, I know." Millie gratefully turned back to Cassie. "I seen yer both at the theater. That is how I knew where to find yer. I also heard yer askin' fer Nell Maggert."

Cassie felt her heart give a tiny leap. Perhaps her daring excursion through the dangerous streets had not been a thorough waste.

"Will you have a seat?" Cassie led the way to the red sofa, watching the girl anxiously perch on the edge of the cushion. At the same moment, the butler entered with a large tray. "Oh, Tolson, please just set that here."

With stiff precision the servant marched to place the tray onto the lacquer table.

"Will there be anything else, my lady?"

"Thank you, no."

Tolson bowed. "Very good."

Not wishing to be overheard by the butler, Cassie busied herself with pouring her guest a cup of tea and filling a china plate with a generous serving of the various sandwiches and pastries. Once the door to the salon had been closed, she offered the delicacies to her guest.

"Oh, it's lovely," Millie breathed.

Sensing the girl was unaccustomed to such a treat, Cassie pretended an interest in preparing Lord Mumford's tea and carrying it across the room to him, determinedly ignoring his sardonic expression. Only when

113

the entire plate of food had been demolished did Cassie return to the sofa and regard Millie with a firm gaze.

"Now, I believe you have some information concerning Nell?"

A wary expression settled on the round face. "Miss Maggert ain't be in no trouble?"

"No, certainly not," Cassie hastily assured. "I merely wish to speak with her."

"Why?"

"It concerns an acquaintance of hers."

Without warning, Luke straightened from the mantel, his dark features set in stern lines.

"How do you know Nell?"

Millie flinched at the abrupt question. "I be her maid."

"Indeed?"

"Yes."

The blue eyes narrowed. "Rather odd for a maid to be at that theater so early in the morning."

Millie jerkily set aside the plate and teacup. "Miss Maggert left behind a shawl that she be particularly fond of. She asked me to fetch it fer her."

"And did she also send you here today?"

"No." There was no mistaking the flare of fear that rippled over the broad countenance. "I ain't said a word about Lady Greer."

114

The dark features sharpened. "And why is that?"

"I . . . I thought . . . that is . . ." Clearly unnerved by Lord Mumford's relentless questions, Millie struggled to meet the glittering gaze.

"You hoped that Lady Greer might be grateful enough for information concerning Nell Maggert that she would offer you a reward?"

The maid jumped to her feet with a stricken expression.

"What if I did? I ain't done nothing wrong."

"No one said that you had," Cassie soothed, rising to her feet. She spared one warning glare to the imposing Lord Mumford before turning back toward the wary maid. "Will you take me to Miss Maggert?"

"I ain't sure . . ." The girl hedged.

"I can pay you for any help you might give."

Millie wavered. "And Miss Maggert won't get hurt?"

"Certainly not."

"Miss Maggert has been good to me."

Cassie smiled in what she hoped was a reassuring manner. "I just have a few questions."

"Well, a girl has to think of her future,"

the maid muttered, twisting the faded skirt with nervous fingers.

"Yes, indeed."

There was a long pause as Millie struggled to overcome her conscience.

"All right, then." She succumbed to temptation, her face pale. "Meet me tomorrow behind the mews. It ain't far from here."

Cassie felt a sharp flare of disappointment. She had wasted a fortnight in this terrible neighborhood. She did not want to waste another moment.

"Can we not go now?" she demanded.

"Oh, no." Millie gave a firm shake of her head. "Miss Maggert be . . . entertaining."

Cassie's face flamed with color as Lord Mumford gave a choked cough that was suspiciously close to a laugh.

"Oh."

"I will meet you at half past ten." The maid appeared unaware of Cassie's discomfort. "I always take the dog for a walk then."

Realizing that there was nothing she could do but wait until the morrow, Cassie gave a reluctant nod.

"Very well," she conceded. "May I offer you more tea?"

"No. I have to get back afore I be missed."

"Of course."

Ignoring Lord Mumford who stood silently beside the mantel, Cassie led the maid out of the room and to the front door.

"Thank you for coming, Miss Stone."

"Yer won't forget tomorrow?"

Cassie could not prevent a wry smile. "Have no fear, I shall not forget."

With a hasty bow, Millie slipped out of the door. Cassie watched as the maid hurried down the path, glancing nervously over her shoulder as if she feared she might be followed.

Cassie slowly shut the door. Tomorrow. Was it possible that she would at last discover Nell? That she at last be given the opportunity to ask the questions that had burned in the back of her mind since her home had been invaded?

There would be no point in becoming overly optimistic, she warned herself.

This Nell Maggert might not even be the Nell she was searching for. Or if she was, she might refuse to admit she was acquainted with Liza. Or it was even possible Millie Stone was lying about her knowledge of Nell and was simply hoping for a few easy quid.

But she at least had hope, and that was more than she possessed a few short hours before.

With a faint sigh, Cassie turned to make her way back to the salon. She had no doubt that Lord Mumford would be waiting eagerly to demand an explanation for the extraordinary encounter. He would also demand to know her interest in Nell Maggert.

Annoying man.

Entering the salon, Cassie prepared herself to fend off the inevitable curiosity. But stepping through the open door, she came to an abrupt halt as she realized the room was empty. A sudden frown marred her brow. It was too much to hope that he had actually disappeared as unexpectedly as he had appeared. So what the devil was he up to now?

Torn between using the opportunity to escape to the safety of her room and the reluctance to appear a coward, Cassie found the decision taken out of her hands as Lord Mumford nonchalantly strolled through the door behind her.

Thoroughly unnerved by his casual manner of wandering through her home, Cassie regarded him with suspicion.

"Do you always pry through people's homes behind their backs?"

He answered her accusation with a vague shrug. Then, withdrawing a delicate snuffbox, he helped himself to a small sample. She watched in burning frustration as he ensured his cuffs were perfectly straight before slowly lifting his head to regard her with a knowing smile.

"I presume it would be a waste of breath to assure you that only a fool would follow a strange woman through the back streets of London?"

Expecting questions, accusations or even threats, Cassie was caught off guard by his wry taunt. For goodness sakes, did the man assume she was a thorough ninny? she wondered. Only desperation would force her into such ridiculous follies.

"As much a waste of breath as me reminding you that what I choose to do is none of your concern," she retaliated with a tilt of her chin.

An unexpectedly wicked grin softened the finely chiseled features.

"Perhaps we are both in need of another lesson," he drawled.

Something perilously close to excitement flared through Cassie even as she took a hasty step backward. She'd had all the lessons she could endure for one day.

"You stay where you are, sir."

The dark head tilted back as he gave a sudden laugh. "Ah, Lady Greer, you are a delight," he said. "Unfortunately, I must take my leave. My aunt has demanded my presence for dinner. Unlike you, she appears to appreciate my charms."

Futilely wishing that Lord Mumford did not possess such an extraordinary ability to unsettle her, Cassie eyed him in a sour manner.

"Is she perfectly well?"

"To the best of my knowledge." His smile widened. "Although my uncle has been known to disagree."

"Well, please do not let me detain you, my lord."

His bow was mockingly elaborate. "A pleasure as always, my lady."

With a last smile, he crossed to disappear out of the French doors. Cassie slowly raised a hand to her pounding heart.

Never would she become accustomed to the dangerous gentleman.

Never.

The town house of Lord and Lady Pembroke was a resplendent testament to the ingenuity of Edward Wyatt. Ornate gilding provided a rich contrast to the deep blue velvet wall coverings throughout the vast rooms, along with pier glass fitted to the doors. The lavish style was echoed in the glittering chandeliers and ebony and gilt furnishings.

Not that Luke was allowed to admire the expensive decor. As was the fashion, Lady Pembroke had invited far more guests than could comfortably squeeze into the house. Climbing the marble staircase, Luke suppressed a grimace at the heat and smoke that greeted him.

Why the devil did a London hostess presume that the more uncomfortable their guests, the more successful their gathering?

It was little wonder a reasonable gentleman preferred the comfort of his club, Luke acknowledged even as he summoned a smile for the thin, silver-haired matron holding court on the landing.

Lady Pembroke was the sister to Luke's late mother and had been a celebrated beauty in her time. A shrewd woman with a taste for comfort, she had chosen a husband who was as rich as he was undemanding. The marriage had flourished remarkably well. Lord Pembroke was allowed his freedom to indulge in his studies of ancient Greek culture, while Lady Pembroke was given an ample income to become a most celebrated hostess. The only blemish on the union was their lack of children.

As a result, Sophia had turned her maternal instincts to the orphanages of London, showering them with both her time and fortune. Her generosity had made her a favorite with Luke, who often added his own wealth to her philanthropic efforts.

Now her thin face lit with surprised pleasure at the sight of him.

"Luke."

He bowed over her outstretched hand. "Aunt Sophia, as beautiful as ever."

"Whatever brings you here?"

Luke straightened to regard her with a teasing smile. "I was invited, was I not?"

"You know quite well you are always invited to our modest gatherings," she retorted, eyeing him in a speculative manner. "However, until this evening you have made a pointed effort to avoid them."

"How shameless of me." Luke lifted his quizzing glass to survey the exquisites that were crowded into the open rooms. "Of course, I was quite unaware how delightful a hostess you are."

"Fah." A cunning lady who did not suffer fools gladly, Sophia met Luke's glittering gaze squarely. "What do you want, Luke?"

"Why, Aunt Sophia. Surely you do not consider me such a shocking bore as to pay my respects only when I require something?"

"That is precisely what I think. I also think that you are far too accustomed to having others pander to your every whim," she retorted in dry tones.

Luke made an unconscious grimace. "Not everyone."

"Indeed?" Sophia gave a surprised blink. "I should like to meet the rare individual willing to dare your displeasure."

Luke suppressed a laugh. He had no doubt Sophia would take great delight in Miss Cassandra Stanholte and her habit of treating him as no more than an unwelcome interloper. For now, however, he intended to keep his intimate knowledge of the young lady a close secret.

"I shall introduce you as soon as she arrives in London," he promised.

"She?" Clearly caught off guard, Sophia grasped his arm to lead him into a nearby alcove. "I demand to know who she is."

Satisfied that he had suitably piqued his aunt's curiosity, Luke gave a mild shrug.

"Miss Cassandra Stanholte."

"Stanholte?" Sophia frowned as she attempted to place the name.

"She currently resides in Devonshire, but she has plans to travel to London for the Season."

The wide eyes became even wider. Hardly

surprising, considering Luke's notorious distaste for debutantes.

"And what is your particular interest in this Miss Stanholte?"

Luke once again shrugged. "Nothing more than a promise to a friend."

"Oh?"

"I assured my dear friend I would see Miss Stanholte comfortably established in a proper town house with a suitable companion," he lied with casual ease.

"You?" Sophia regarded him in blatant disbelief. "Absurd."

Luke smiled in wry amusement. "Why?"

"What do you possibly know of settling a young lady in a proper establishment?" Sophia demanded.

"Thankfully, not a whit," Luke confessed, absently smoothing the fold of his intricately knotted cravat. For the occasion he had chosen a black satin coat and pantaloons with a snow white waistcoat. A large ruby glinted against his lapel. Oddly, the severe attire only enhanced the masculine form and darkly handsome features. A fact that was noted by the vast majority of the females throughout the room. "Which is precisely why I have come to you."

"You wish me to rent an establishment?" Sophia frowned in puzzlement.

"Actually, I plan to have my secretary make the necessary inquiries for a town house." Luke waved a negligent hand. He could hardly confess he had personally met with an agent today to choose a town house that would suit his very high demands. "What I need from you is a gently bred lady who would agree to act as a chaperon for the remainder of the Season."

For a long moment his aunt studied his carefully bland countenance, as if seeking to determine the truth behind his decidedly queer behavior. Luke held his breath. He was going to need the support of Lady Pembroke if his plan to remove Miss Stanholte to a respectable establishment was to succeed.

"I do have a school friend who has fallen upon difficult times," she at last confessed. "She is currently residing with her brother, a boorish prig whom she will no doubt be delighted to escape, but she is bound to be curious why I should take such an inordinate amount of interest in an unknown Miss straight from the country." Sophia lifted her brow in a meaningful gesture. "As will all of London."

Luke was well aware of the risk of scandal. Still, what choice did he have? He could hardly allow Miss Stanholte to remain in her current home.

"I shall rely upon your discretion to avoid any unwelcome gossip," he responded, his tone somber.

Sophia tilted her head to one side. "I do not suppose I can convince you to tell me the truth?"

As swiftly as it had disappeared, his lazy smile returned. "Whatever do you mean, Aunt Sophia?"

"I may be old, Luke, but I am not entirely beetle-witted," Sophia pointed out in dry tones. "No gentleman, friend or otherwise, would entrust a susceptible debutante to the care of a noted rake."

Luke could not resist a low chuckle. "Why, Aunt Sophia, I am deeply shocked."

"Fah." She lightly batted him with her fan, even as her gaze narrowed with suspicion. "This lady is . . . respectable?"

It was Luke's turn to be caught off guard. "Do you believe I would attempt to foist my mistress onto Society?"

Sophia shrugged. "It has been known to occur."

"I assure you, the lady is beyond reproach."

Luke was once more subjected to that searching, rather quizzical glance.

"I must admit I am intrigued, Luke."

"Then you will lend me your aid?"

The older woman gave a sudden decisive nod of her head. "I will visit Anne Stowe and inquire if she will be willing to become a chaperon."

Luke felt a flare of relief at her agreement. With a town house secured and a chaperon discovered, he was quite confident that he would have Miss Stanholte established within a few days. If only he could keep her from blundering into some disaster before then.

"I knew I could depend upon you, Aunt Sophia." He offered her a roguish grin. "Of all my large and usually tiresome family, you are beyond a doubt my favorite."

Waving aside his absurd compliment, Sophia regarded him with a simmering curiosity.

"Tell me about this Miss Stanholte," she demanded.

His smile twisted with a hint of self-mockery. "She is beautiful, intelligent and occasionally charming," he obligingly described. "She is also a lady of staunch independence who considers me a deplorable cad."

Sophia's laughter chimed over the muted din of the guests. "Good for her. I believe I like her already."

Taking his aunt's hand, he bowed with exquisite grace. "Now I believe I shall take myself to the card room and sample Uncle Henry's fine brandy. Pray contact me after you have spoken with Miss Stowe."

Leaving Lady Pembroke regarding him in a most suspicious manner, Luke made his way through the chattering guests to a back salon. He would pay his respects to his uncle and take his leave.

He had achieved what he wanted.

Seven

A layer of thick clouds hung over the city as Cassie waited in the shadows of the mews. The brooding grayness only added to her sense of unease, and with a shiver she pulled the thick cloak closer about her tense frame.

Not for the first time she wondered if she was once again behaving like a fool. Would any lady with the least sense be standing alone in this neighborhood waiting for a perfect stranger?

After all, Lord Mumford had been quite correct when he had warned that Millie might very well be leading her into a trap.

No, she fiercely told herself. She would not think of Lord Mumford. Not now.

It was bad enough that she had endured a sleepless night reliving those moments in his arms over and over. And that she could still smell the scent of sandalwood lingering in her salon. She would not have him haunt her every moment.

Twitching her cloak even tighter, Cassie peered down the foggy lane. It was well past the appointed time, and she was beginning to fear that Millie was not going to show. Regardless of her doubts, Millie was her only lead. If the young maid did not appear, she would have nothing.

Intent on the path, Cassie took little heed of the faint rustle in a distant hedge. It wasn't until a thin form abruptly pushed its way through the hedge and stepped into view that she turned with a small gasp.

Her heart gave a sharp leap of dismay. She easily recognized the thin, unpleasant features of the man from the theater. Toby? Yes, that was his name.

She stepped backward, but at the same moment another figure emerged from behind her. This time she did not recognize the large, broad-faced man, but it was obvious he was as dangerous as his companion. With an effort, Cassie suppressed her instinctive scream. She couldn't panic. It was essential she keep her wits about her.

"Ah, Lady Greer." Toby performed a mocking bow, clearly enjoying her startled expression. "What a pleasure."

Cassie tilted a determined chin. She would not give this man the satisfaction of seeing her inner fear.

"What do you want, Toby?"

Toby smirked as he strolled closer. "Millie sends her regrets, but she was unable to meet you today."

Something in his tone made Cassie's

heart take another leap. Oh, dear heavens, what had she gotten herself into?

"Where is Millie?"

"Never mind about her," he growled. "Yer just come along nicely and yer won't get hurt."

"What have you done with Millie?" she shrilly demanded, too frightened to even consider her own plight.

"I gave her a coin and sent her on her way. Far better than you are going to get," Toby promised in an evil tone.

"No —"

"Grab her," Toby ordered his silent companion.

Suddenly jolted into the realization that these two men intended to forcibly kidnap her, Cassie attempted to turn back to the small gate that led to her grounds. If only she could get close enough, a scream might alert the staff to her danger. But even as she stumbled over the hem of her cloak, rough arms were encircling her body and hauling her against a hard man's frame.

Cassie nearly gagged as the vile odors of whiskey and an unwashed body clouded the air.

"Let me go," she gritted, kicking her foot backward in the hope of hitting a knee.

Toby slipped forward, pulling a knife

from beneath his shabby coat.

"I suggest yer stop fighting. Yer wouldn't want that pretty face hurt, would yer?"

A chill of sheer terror raced down her spine. "I will scream," she threatened, knowing the threat was futile even before Toby gave a sharp laugh.

"There be no one but the rats to hear yer screams, my lady."

"What do you want from me?"

"All in good time." Toby gave a jerk of his head. "Let's go."

"I fear you will not be going anywhere," a third male voice suddenly drawled as the elegant Lord Bidwell stepped out of the fog.

Cassie felt a flare of relief as Toby spun about to regard the gentleman outrageously attired in a shocking yellow coat with a red striped waistcoat.

"What the bloody hell?" Toby cursed in frustration. "This ain't yer business, guv."

"You are mistaken." Yet another male voice answered, this one all too familiar to Cassie. All heads turned as Lord Mumford rounded the corner of the mews holding a pistol. "This is very much our business."

"You," the thin man breathed.

Lord Mumford smiled without humor. "I suspected that I would find you here this morning, Toby."

A flash of fear narrowed the close-set eyes as Toby raised his hands, the knife thumping onto the damp ground.

"I ain't meant no harm. I only wished to talk with Her Ladyship."

The smile twisted with sardonic disbelief. "You can explain that to the magistrate."

The mention of the magistrate had a startling effect on the two men. With a muffled curse, the scoundrel holding Cassie shoved her aside and plunged back into the nearby hedge. At the same moment, Toby darted behind his lumbering friend to make his escape.

"Biddles," Lord Mumford called as he hastily moved to Cassie's side.

The tiny gentleman rolled his eyes heavenward in resignation.

"Why do you not chase the villains through the nasty streets of London while I remain with the beautiful damsel in distress?"

"Biddles." Luke flashed his friend a warning glare.

"Very well." Biddles performed an elegant bow. "Adieu, my lady."

With startling agility, the nobleman withdrew a silver pistol from his coat and in a blink disappeared into the hedge. Cassie watched him with a vague sense of unreality, suddenly aware that her head was swimming in a most alarming fashion.

"Oh."

As always, Lord Mumford appeared to read her very thoughts. Without a word, he bent downward, scooping her up in his arms as if she weighed no more than a child. Unfortunately, her reaction to his close proximity was anything but childlike.

Being pressed so intimately against the broad chest reminded her vividly of their embrace of the day before. Once again her body trembled as a rash of awareness tingled over her skin. Moments before, she had been filled with terror; now that terror was slowly receding and a delicious heat was flowing through her blood.

Clenching her eyes shut, Cassie attempted to control the flutters of pleasure stirring deep inside her. It was a futile effort. She was only more aware of the slender hands cradling her with exquisite care and the tantalizing scent of his warm skin.

How could this man disturb her with a mere touch? She was no susceptible chit to swoon over every handsome gentleman. It was all so annoyingly unfair.

For a long moment she battled the absurd desire to relax against the strength of his enticing male form, barely aware that his long strides had taken them back through the gate and up the path to the house. It was only when he bent forward to pull open the French door that she forced her eyes open.

"My lord, I insist that you put me down," she demanded, her voice oddly breathless.

The blue eyes lowered to her flushed countenance, smoldering with an emotion that made her shiver.

"Not now, Miss Stanholte," he warned. "I am in little humor for your shrewish independence."

Shrewish? Why, the rotten toad. She was not a shrew.

"I am perfectly capable of walking."

"Just as you are perfectly capable of taking care of yourself?" he taunted, abruptly lowering her onto the sofa. The sensation of his satin hair brushing her mouth stole her tart reply as he moved across the room and then swiftly returned to shove a crystal glass into her hand. "Here."

Cassie warily regarded the amber liquid. "What is it?"

"Brandy." Standing over her, Luke crossed his arms over the width of his chest. "Hardly the finest, but it will have to do."

Willing to try anything if it would ease the tension gripping her body, Cassie took a cautious sip. At once she gave a choked cough, her eyes flooding with tears.

"Good heavens. You drink this?"

"On occasion." His stern expression never faltered. "Finish it."

Disliking his imperious command, Cassie impulsively raised the glass and tossed the fiery liquid down her throat in one motion. A trail of fire burned its way to the pit of her stomach, but she grimly refused to allow herself more than a small shudder. Setting aside the glass, she frowned at him with a stubborn expression.

"You needn't stand there glaring at me in that superior fashion."

A raven brow slowly raised. "You are fortunate that I do not reward such absurdly childish behavior in the manner it deserves."

"You have no right to do anything with me, my lord," she tartly reminded him, setting aside the glass. She was beginning to realize that Lord Mumford had planned this ambush since Millie's arrival yesterday. She had been a simpleton to believe he would allow her to handle her own affairs. "I certainly did not request your interference."

His smile was without humor. "And yet you appeared remarkably relieved to see me."

Did he have to be so bloody conde-

scending? she wondered with unladylike irritation.

"What do you wish from me?" she demanded. "My gratitude?"

He gave a sharp laugh as he shook his
head. "I would not ask for the impossible.
No, what I wish from you is the truth."

"Truth?"

His expression hardened. "Why are you
searching for Nell Maggert?"

Still reeling from the various shocks of the
morning, Cassie found herself floundering
beneath his narrowed gaze. Why, oh, why
hadn't she suspected this inquisition was
coming?

"I wish to speak with her."

"Why?"

"I . . . I am acquainted with a friend of
hers."

"Balderdash," he retorted in patent disbelief.

Unable to withstand his piercing scrutiny,
Cassie abruptly rose to her feet.

"I appreciate your assistance, my lord,
but I must request that you take your leave
now."

With a deliberate motion he stepped
closer, his expression grim.

"Not until you have answered my questions."

Her heart faltered, a sense of impending disaster suddenly filling the air. He appeared so very sure she would confess.

"I have no intention of answering your questions," she bravely attempted to bluff. "Now or ever."

"Oh, I believe you will, Lady Greer," he drawled. "Or do you prefer Miss Stanholte?"

Just for a moment she convinced herself that she could not have heard correctly. No matter how clever Lord Mumford might be, there was no means of his discovering her true identity. Unless Mrs. Green had revealed their secret, which was as likely as the sky falling.

"What?"

"Miss Cassandra Stanholte," he obligingly repeated, closely watching her horrified expression. "From Devonshire."

So it was true. Somehow Lord Mumford had managed to learn who she was, and her worst fears were about to be realized. Unconsciously, Cassie lifted a hand to her quaking heart.

"How could you possibly know?"

"I will admit that you did not make it simple." A slow, devilishly charming smile softened his stern features. "But I have always found a challenge to be quite irresistible."

"Oh . . ." She abruptly turned from the disturbing blue eyes. "Why could you not have left me in peace?"

She felt rather than heard him move to stand directly behind her, his hands gently reaching up to slip off the heavy cloak. Cassie shivered, although she was uncertain if it was due to the cool air penetrating her thin muslin gown or the lingering touch of his fingers.

"If I had left you in peace, you no doubt would now be in the clutches of the charming Toby."

She could hardly argue with such a legitimate accusation, so instead she turned her attention to her most pressing fear.

"What do you intend to do?"

"I will explain all in good time," he parried with his usual skill; then his hands firmly turned her about to face his searching gaze. "But first you will answer my questions."

Cassie instinctively pulled away from his unnerving touch.

"What do you wish to know?"

"Why did you come to London?"

Cassie hesitated. She wanted to fabricate some plausible story. To divert him from the truth. But as a woman renowned for her forthright honesty, she found it ridiculously difficult to conjure a suitable lie.

At last she heaved a small sigh of resignation. "Several weeks ago a strange woman arrived at my estate with a small boy. This woman claimed to have married my uncle who disappeared from England before I was ever born. She also claimed that the boy was the legitimate heir to the Stanholte title and estate."

He was silent for long minutes as he considered her abrupt explanation. Then his raven brows pulled together.

"Surely you did not simply accept her claim?"

"Of course not." Cassie gave a restless shrug. "But she has been very clever. On the surface, her documents appear genuine. It could be years before my Man of Business proves that she is a fraud."

There was another long silence as his gaze probed her wide eyes.

"And you are quite certain she is a fraud?"

Cassie never hesitated. "Without a doubt."

Surprisingly, he seemed to accept her assurance without question, giving a decisive nod of his head.

"Very well." His gaze narrowed. "That still does not explain your presence in the neighborhood."

Her nose flared with mounting ill temper. Must he know every sordid detail?

It appeared he did, and with jerky steps Cassie crossed to the mantel where she pulled a crumpled note from a small vase. Turning about, she returned to the watchful Lord Mumford and thrust it into his hand.

"Here."

With a frown, the gentleman unfolded the note and scanned the sprawling handwriting.

"Ah . . ." He slowly lifted his head, his expression wry. "So that explains your fascination with women named Nell. What do you hope to accomplish by finding her?"

Cassie bristled at his tone. He need not regard her as if she were a particularly dimwitted child.

"I will demand that she confess Liza is not Lady Stanholte."

"I see," he murmured. "And you believe she will simply comply with your request?"

"If I threaten her with the magistrate," she retorted with a tilt of her chin.

"She is far more likely to have a knife slipped into your back."

Her face paled as the thrust hit its target. It was true. Thus far her efforts had done no more than place her in continuing danger. Still, she was in no humor to admit the truth. At least not to Lord Mumford.

"My lord, that is enough —"

"No, Miss Stanholte," he interrupted in stern tones. "For once, you will listen to what I have to say." He planted his hands firmly on his hips. "Not only have you risked your reputation with this absurd scheme, but you are quite fortunate not to have been grievously injured."

Her expression became unconsciously petulant. "I presume you are in agreement with Mr. Carson, who believes I should meekly stand aside while this impostor steals my inheritance?"

"Certainly not," he denied. "But that does not mean I approve of this dangerous charade."

Outside, the blanket of clouds parted to allow a brief spray of sunshine into the salon. The golden warmth reflected off the satin darkness of his hair and outlined the magnificence of his profile. Cassie struggled to keep her gaze from lingering.

"I do not need your approval."

He gave a low, decidedly unnerving chuckle. "Unfortunately, you do. Unless you wish the world to know that the lovely Lady Greer is in reality Miss Stanholte."

She sucked in a sharp breath. "You wouldn't."

"You leave me little choice." He gave a faint shrug. "I cannot in all good conscience leave you in this house to continue your ridiculous game. And if exposing your identity is the only means of saving you from your own foolishness then that is precisely what I shall be doing."

Cassie felt a ridiculous stab of disappointment. Perhaps naively, she had thought he might be different from the rest of the frippery *ton* and he would understand her need to save her home.

"You forget I have nowhere else to go," she gritted, determined to hide her moment of weakness.

"Actually, you have a very nice establishment waiting."

"What?"

"It is not particularly large, but it appears to be well proportioned and possesses a fully trained staff. Best of all, it is situated close to the park."

Cassie shook her head. "I haven't the least notion what you are talking about."

He smiled at her baffled expression. "I have rented a town house for you. I have also requested that my aunt select a suitable companion to reside with you."

Barely aware she was moving, Cassie weakly collapsed onto a nearby chair. Once, her life had been tediously predictable, each day much like another. Now she seemed to tumble from one shock to another.

"How dare you?" she breathed.

"How dare I what?" he demanded without apology. "Remove you from a notorious neighborhood? Save you from the likes of Toby? Provide you with the means of remaining in London?"

Cassie flinched as his words struck to her very heart. Somehow he always managed to make his interference appear perfectly reasonable. Even something as outrageous as renting her a town house.

"Why? Why would you do this? I am nothing to you."

Assuming the bland nonchalance she detested, Lord Mumford carefully adjusted the cuff of his pearl gray coat.

"Because it suits me," he said simply.

"Well it does not suit me, my lord," Cassie gritted. "I came to London to save my estate, not to languish in a well-appointed establishment, with or without a view of the park."

Quite unperturbed by her flare of temper, Luke met her glittering gaze squarely.

"I assure you that your estate will be saved even if you are in a respectable neighborhood."

"I can hardly search for Nell once I am no longer here," she pointed out. Really, did this gentleman presume she could be distracted from her task by dangling an elegant town house before her nose?

"Precisely." The handsome features abruptly hardened. "Your search for Nell comes to an end as of this moment. From now on, any search will be my responsibility."

For a moment she merely glared at him, longing to defy his arrogant commands. He had no right to order her about in such a manner. But the knowledge that he could bring her entire charade to a scandalous halt held her unruly tongue.

It appeared that for now Lord Mumford held the reins firmly in hand. She would have to bide her time for retribution.

What a glorious day that would be.

"And what am I to do?" she at last managed to demand.

He smiled as if sensing the effort it cost her to remain civil.

"You are to enjoy the delights of the Season."

She didn't bother to hide her grimace. "You realize that once it becomes known that you were responsible for renting the town house, I shall be the center of gossip?"

145

"You may be assured that no one will suspect."

Cassie fully believed him. The beastly man appeared infallible.

"It appears I have little option," she sulked.

"None at all. Please be prepared to move by the end of the week. I will speak with my aunt and ensure that your companion is installed before then."

"You seem to have taken care of everything."

His lips quirked as his gaze moved over her in a slow survey.

"Not everything. I would suggest that you consider a more . . . modest wardrobe. As well as a return of those charming golden curls."

Cassie's initial embarrassment at his intimate regard was sharply thrust aside by a stab of horrified disbelief.

Golden curls.

She hadn't fooled him at all. The entire time she had thought she was being so clever, he had known she was the bedraggled Miss who had collapsed beneath his carriage.

"Why, you . . . you have known all along, haven't you?"

He shrugged aside her question. "I will

contact you when all is prepared." He bowed. "Until then, Miss Stanholte."

She gave a frosty nod of her head, determined to maintain at least a semblance of composure. She knew quite well that to give rein to her frustration would only damage her pride. It would certainly not sway Lord Mumford into being remotely reasonable.

Her determination lasted until Lord Mumford had turned to disappear through the French doors; then she impulsively grasped a hideous figurine and launched it into the fireplace. The resounding crash did little to ease her simmering tension, although it did bring the rotund figure of Mary Green scurrying into the room.

Half an hour too late, Cassie thought unfairly.

"Miss Cassie, has something occurred?" Mary demanded with a worried frown.

"Lord Mumford is what has occurred, Mary." Cassie rose to her feet. "Why will he not leave us alone?"

Glancing in a knowing manner at the broken figurine, Mary allowed a smile to touch her round face.

"I should very much like to know myself, Miss Cassie."

Eight

Leaving the house, Luke made his way back to the mews. He barely noted the drizzling rain as he gathered the reins of his black stallion and those of Biddles's gray. His gaze moved to the spot where Miss Stanholte had been standing.

His heart had nearly halted when he had seen her being so roughly handled by the brutal blackguard. And then Toby had pulled a knife. . . .

Luke shuddered, wrenching his thoughts from that terrible moment.

It had all seemed so cunning when he and Biddles had devised the plan the night before. They would wait in the hedges for Millie to appear and then follow them to whatever trap had been laid. It had not occurred to him that Toby would be bold enough to attempt to kidnap Miss Stanholte so close to her own home.

Lost in his dark thoughts, Luke was startled as the slender gentleman suddenly appeared from the hedges.

"Egad, do not say the chit had you tossed into this weather?" Biddles drawled, languidly moving to join Luke. "Really,

Mumford, I fear your reputation as an irresistible rake is in decided peril."

"Very amusing." Luke tossed his companion the reins to the gray. "At least I did not allow a mere cutpurse to give me the slip."

Biddles offered him a pained expression of outrage.

"Hardly the slip, old chap. I followed the little bugger to a particularly nasty theater. Prudence forced me to return for reinforcements before entering."

"A theater, eh?" Luke nodded, already having suspected Toby would flee to his seeming hideout.

"Do you know the place?"

"Unfortunately." Luke grimaced as he smoothly vaulted into the saddle of his waiting mount. "Shall we discover what our friend has to say for himself?"

Biddles heaved a long-suffering sigh as he too took to the saddle.

"I feared you might say as much. I do hope that on the next occasion you choose a mistress, Mumford, you choose one who does not require such constant care."

Urging his horse forward, Luke smiled in a wry fashion. "I shall contrive to do my best," he promised.

Together they traveled through the wet

streets of London, both on guard in the event Toby was plotting yet another surprise. On this occasion, however, there were no unpleasant traps, and they pulled to a halt in front of the theater.

In the dull light the shabby building appeared even more forlorn, and Biddles cast Luke a wary glance.

"Perhaps we should take ourselves to the back entrance?"

"Excellent notion, Biddles." Luke slid off the stallion and tied off the reins. "No sense announcing our presence."

"No, indeed." The foppish gentleman joined him, and with considerable stealth they edged their way to the back entrance. Both grimaced at the stench of rotting garbage and things less easily identified. Luke had no doubt his boots would be ruined beyond repair, but for the moment he was far more concerned with pushing open the wooden door and peering into the dark room within.

The stench inside was not a noticeable improvement, and it was quickly obvious the back room was used to house a number of ruffians.

Tattered blankets, dirty crockery and an empty keg of ale were littered on one side of the room, while the other was piled with numerous mounds of costumes. Across the room, an open door revealed a set of stairs leading to the main floor.

Cautiously entering the room, Luke scrutinized his surroundings. Behind him, Biddles gave a disapproving sniff.

"It appears the scoundrel has made his escape."

Luke shrugged, his eyes narrowing as he caught sight of a crumpled note lying beside the fire grate.

"What have we here?" he murmured, moving to pick up the partially burned letter.

He gave a low whistle as he read the nearly incoherent missive from Liza. In it she pleaded to return to London and complained that the neighbors in Devonshire treated her in a shabby fashion. She also insisted that she feared Miss Stanholte suspected that she was a fraud and meant to see her thrown to the magistrate. Annoyingly, any hint as to whom she had sent the letter to had been burned away. Still, the note at least confirmed he was on the right track. Turning, he handed the letter to his companion.

"It appears that Liza is becoming increasingly nervous in her role as Lady Stanholte."

Biddles frowned. "Liza?"

As concisely as possible, Luke revealed the secret behind Miss Stanholte's arrival in London and her determination to unmask the intruder posing as Lady Stanholte. Biddles listened in silence as Luke at last pointed toward the letter.

"Now we can be certain this Toby is involved in the scheme to steal Miss Stanholte's inheritance."

Handing the letter back to Luke, the smaller man pursed his lips in a thoughtful manner.

"No doubt he is involved," Biddles agreed. "But he did not impress me as a particularly intelligent chap. I should be very much surprised if he managed to invent such a scheme on his own."

Intent on the letter, Luke abruptly stiffened as the sound of approaching footsteps echoed eerily through the room. With a sharp movement of one hand, Biddles pointed toward a mound of costumes. Moving with silent speed, the two quickly secreted themselves behind the mildewed clothing, barely out of sight before the footsteps entered the room.

Shifting to one side, Luke carefully peered around the costumes, easily recognizing the thin form of Toby. Luke was unfamiliar, however, with the tall, surprisingly well-attired gentleman with him. He took careful note of the fashionably styled brown hair and the narrow countenance marred by a thin scar down one cheek. Not a face easily forgotten.

Impatiently tapping a riding crop against a glossy boot, the stranger paced the room with obvious anger.

"Can I not trust you to follow a simple command?" he demanded in an educated voice, distinctly at odds with his surroundings.

"Ain't my fault those blokes appeared," Toby whined.

The tall gentleman glared down his long nose.

"Really, Crumby, your excuses are becoming as tiresome as your incompetence. Is it so difficult to bring me one small chit?"

Luke and Biddles exchanged a knowing glance. Clearly, they had discovered the leader behind Miss Stanholte's troubles.

"If it be so easy, why don't yer get her yerself?" Toby sulked.

"Because, my dim-witted friend, that is what I have paid you to do." The soft voice was menacing. "A payment I shall take out in blood if you do not succeed."

Even from a distance, Luke could see

Toby stiffen in fear. Clearly, Toby recognized the danger etched in the gentleman's narrow countenance.

"Yer needn't threaten me," the smaller man attempted to bluster. "I'll have the lady by tomorrow."

Without warning, the riding crop cracked across the top of a scarred table.

"Do not be any more of a fool than you have to be, Crumby," he snarled. "These two mysterious gentlemen are clearly aware of your interest in Lady Greer. What do you suppose would happen if she were to suddenly disappear?"

Toby flinched, his grimy face becoming pale. "What do yer want me to do?"

There was a brief silence as the gentleman resumed his pacing, obviously pondering how best to proceed. At last he halted and turned back to the cowering Toby.

"Nothing for now," he commanded. "I shall have to devise a more subtle means of ridding myself of the pesky Miss Stanholte. One that can be passed as nothing more sinister than an unfortunate accident. I have no need for unwelcome questions." Luke felt his blood freeze at the icy tone. The stranger was clearly devoid of conscience or emotion. "Until then you are to remain here. You have done enough damage with your blundering."

Laying the crop against Toby's white face in a taunting manner, the gentleman gave a contemptuous laugh. Then, certain he had suitably cowed his incompetent thug, he slowly strolled out of the room and up the stairs.

For a long moment Toby eyed the retreating figure, waiting until he was certain the gentleman was well away from the room before spitting on the straw-covered floor.

"Bloody bastard," he cursed before turning on his heel and defiantly marching out the back door.

Counting to one hundred to ascertain that neither man was about to suddenly reappear, Luke and Biddles slowly moved from behind the costumes. Removing a perfumed bit of satin from his sleeve, Biddles lifted it to his pointed nose.

"Rather detestable sort of bloke." He narrowly gazed toward the stairs. "A friend of yours?"

"No," Luke retorted in a clipped tone, his hands clenched in unconscious fists. "At least he has satisfied my curiosity. We now know who possessed the cunning to devise a campaign to steal Miss Stanholte's inheritance, indeed.

"But who is he? And how the devil are we to stop him?" Luke growled in frustration.

The sense of Miss Stanholte's danger had never been more pressing. The unknown gentleman had revealed a cold, calculated determination to capture his prey, and a thorough lack of scruples that would allow him to do whatever was necessary to achieve his goal. An image of a delicate face with large silver eyes and utterly kissable lips suddenly burned in the front of Luke's mind. No. He would not allow this blackguard to harm a golden hair on her head. Not if he had to hunt the scoundrel from one end of England to another.

"Come along, Biddles. I must ensure that Aunt Sophia has secured Miss Stowe. The sooner Miss Stanholte is out of that neighborhood, the better."

Ten days later, Luke stepped out of the glossy black carriage and crossed to the side of the elegantly situated town house. It was the first occasion he had allowed himself to visit Miss Stanholte since the morning he had revealed to her that he knew the truth behind her deception. Staying away was not an easy task when he was constantly on edge that something would occur in his absence, but the knowledge that all eyes of Society would be trained upon the newly arrived lady and her companion had kept him away.

He wanted no undue speculation about his immediate interest in a country Miss.

Of course, he hadn't left the safety of Miss Stanholte to chance. Even before she had been removed to the house, he had installed a footman in his service. The servant had been commanded to keep a constant guard on the lady and to report anything remotely suspicious. Luke had also devoted his time to scouring the gentlemen's clubs, the gaming hells and brothels in search of the scar-faced gentleman from the theater. Annoyingly, he had caught no sight of the stranger; he was obviously keeping away from the more public entertainments.

Now Luke felt an undeniable surge of anticipation as he moved up the narrow path. He had missed his visits with Miss Stanholte more than he cared to admit, and it had only been with a disturbing effort that he had resisted the temptation to call.

First, however, he had arranged to meet with his trusted servant.

Feigning an interest in the neatly tended roses beside the house, Luke stopped to study a deep red bloom. With the same casual manner, a uniformed footman stepped through a side door and crossed to stand beside Luke.

"My lord." The slender servant with

trimmed brown hair and dark eyes gave a small bow.

"Ramsel." Luke nodded at the younger brother of his own secretary. The Ramsel family had been tenants on his uncle's estate for generations and had proven an unwavering loyalty to the earl. "Any news?"

"I caught sight of one chap staring at the house," he duly reported. "I tried to follow him, but he was a slippery bloke. Lost him a few blocks away."

Luke resisted the urge to jump to the conclusion that the lurker was Toby or his nefarious employer. As a new tenant in the neighborhood, Miss Stanholte was bound to attract the attention of many people. Not all of whom were determined to do her harm.

"How is Miss Stanholte?" he quizzed. "Is she settled in?"

The footman scratched his head as he considered his response.

"Didn't appear a mite happy when she first arrived, but her maid Rose says that she seems to have perked up."

Luke smiled wryly. He could imagine Miss Stanholte's displeasure when she had received his note commanding her to remove to this town house. He had no doubt that he had been called any number of colorful names.

"Have there been any callers?"

"A right number, my lord. 'Course it's not surprising, with Lady Pembroke taking such an interest and Miss Stanholte being such a lovely lady." His youthful features abruptly flushed with painful color. "If you don't mind me saying so, sir."

Luke swiftly eased the young man's embarrassment. "Certainly not. Has there been a tall man with dark hair and a scar down one cheek?"

"Not that I seen." Ramsel shrugged. "Mostly gents like Lord Westwood and Mr. Talvert. In fact, they are with Miss Stanholte this morning."

"Good God, Aunt Sophia did not waste any time," Luke muttered, reaching into his pocket to withdraw a slender envelope. "Thank you, Ramsel. Keep me informed."

The footman accepted the envelope with a bow. "Yes, my lord."

Moving to the front of the house, Luke mounted the stairs. Although he had deliberately requested his aunt to visit Miss Stanholte today so he would possess an excuse to call, he had not expected her to bring Lord Pembroke's tedious cousin, Lord Westwood, and his constant companion. The knowledge that they were frequent visitors brought a frown to his handsome countenance as the elderly butler pulled open the door.

"Lord Mumford to see Miss Stanholte," he commanded.

The thin, nearly bald-headed man waved him into the foyer. "Wait here, my lord."

Luke was kept waiting only a moment before he was stiffly led to the front drawing room. As the butler announced his presence, Luke took a moment to admire his surroundings.

He had known the moment he had viewed the house it would be perfect. The rooms were well situated, with a number of windows and a classic simplicity that was quite lovely. Most charming of all were the delicate landscapes painted throughout the house. Rolling meadows, trees and clouds were offset by a trellis frame, giving the image of gazing upon the English countryside.

Luke had not missed Lady Greer's wistful expression whenever he had spoken of his estate in Kent. It was clear that she missed her own country estate, and he had hoped the pastoral scenes would ease her homesickness.

Having performed his service, the butler stepped aside to allow Luke his first glimpse of Miss Stanholte in ten long days. Even prepared, he felt his heart give a sharp jerk at the sight of her seated on the satinwood and silk sofa.

She was beautiful.

Golden curls were elegantly arranged atop her head, with a handful left to caress the curve of her neck and her soft cheeks. Her gown was pale rose, and while more concealing than her previous attire, the supple muslin managed to cling to the slender curves in the most disturbing fashion. She looked extraordinarily young and innocent, and Luke experienced a most absurd desire to sweep her into his arms and carry her far away.

Decidedly odd behavior for a gentleman who had always branded such romantic nonsense fit for only fribbles and twits.

With an effort, he forced his gaze toward his aunt and the two young dandies seated on a nearby sofa. The three of them regarded him with varying expressions. Lady Pembroke was speculative, while the timid Mr. Talvert appeared struck by being in the presence of the Irresistible Earl. Lord Westwood was simply annoyed at having to share the attention of the lovely Miss Stanholte. Luke's own expression was unreadable as he offered them a graceful leg.

"Aunt Sophia, I was told I could find you here."

"Luke." Lady Pembroke smiled as she lifted a heavily jeweled hand. "I do not believe you have been formally introduced to Miss Stanholte? She is recently come to London and is eager to enjoy the delights of town. Miss Stanholte, may I introduce my nephew, Lord Mumford?"

Swift to take advantage of the opportunity to move closer to Miss Stanholte, Luke crossed to the slender maiden. Ignoring her haughty expression, he deliberately reached down to grasp her stiff fingers and lifted them to his lips. He slowly smiled as he felt her sudden tremor.

"Your servant, Miss Stanholte."

Her eyes flashed silver. Clearly, he was still out of favor.

"My lord."

"And her companion, Miss Stowe," Sophia interrupted their silent exchange, and Luke was forced to turn to acknowledge the small, rather dowdy lady nearly hidden in the corner.

"Miss Stowe," he murmured, feeling a faint twinge of unease. Good God, the woman appeared as if she might swoon at the drop of a pin. How the devil was she to chaperon a spirited minx like Miss Stanholte? Then he met her steady brown eyes, and a portion of his fear eased. Perhaps there was more to the lady than appeared from her subdued manner.

"My lord."

"And, of course, you are acquainted with Lord Pembroke's cousin, Lord Westwood, and his friend, Mr. Talvert."

"Westwood. Talvert." Having performed his social obligations, Luke casually lowered his tall frame onto the sofa next to Miss Stanholte. He conveniently ignored the hiss from Lord Westwood and the raised brow of his aunt. "Tell me, Miss Stanholte, how are you enjoying London?"

Forced by her surroundings to make a pretense of polite civility, Miss Stanholte gave a small tilt of her chin.

"It is all that I expected, my lord."

His mouth twitched at her subtle taunt. "Have you managed to see any of the sights?"

"Lady Pembroke has been kind enough to invite me to visit the Tower of London and the Royal Academy."

"I am attempting to convince her to join my gathering tonight," Lady Pembroke chimed in. "It will be the perfect opportunity to introduce her to Society. And Lord Westwood has promised to perform his latest poem."

Having been unfortunate enough to have

endured the tedious drivel Lord Westwood claimed as poetry, Luke barely swallowed his laugh.

"A delight not be missed. Of course, Miss Stanholte will attend," he drawled, his smile widening as her slim form stiffened.

"Wonderful. Then I shall expect both of you." Sophia easily tumbled Luke into his own trap and then rose with a satisfied expression. "Peter, I am ready to leave."

With obvious reluctance, Lord Westwood rose and crossed to his hostess. Lifting her hand, he spared Luke a small glare before kissing the slender fingers.

"Until this evening, Miss Stanholte," he reverently proclaimed.

Perhaps noting Luke's steely gaze at Lord Westwood's intimate manner, Mr. Talvert contented himself with a distant bow.

"Your servant, Miss Stanholte."

The three made a protracted leave-taking, with Peter returning twice to retrieve Lady Pembroke's fan and a missing glove. At last they were gone, and Luke was left alone with Miss Stanholte and her watchful companion.

Settling back on the sofa, Luke subdued a stab of regret that their days of conversing without the strictures of a proper chaperon were over.

"A charming establishment, Miss Stanholte," he broke the awkward silence, a wicked glint of amusement in his eyes.

She lifted a cool brow. "Indeed? I suppose it is adequate."

"Merely adequate?" His lips twitched, as he was well aware the town house was considered one of the finest in all of London.

"Unfortunately, the upstairs is unaccountably cramped, and there is a dampness in the air I cannot like."

"Ah, at least you can find no fault with the furnishings." He deliberately allowed his gaze to roam the satinwood furniture covered to complement the blues and greens of the landscapes. To one side, a heavy side table with a granite top sported three handsome Greek vases. On a far wall, a delicately scrolled chimneypiece reflected the classic style. "Unless you prefer the latest fashions from the Orient? For myself, I could never abide lacquer."

She could not prevent her blush at his subtle taunt.

"As I said, it is all quite adequate."

He gave a soft laugh. "I perceive that you have caught my aunt's fancy."

"Lady Pembroke has been very kind."

There was no doubting the sincerity in her tone, and Luke smiled with wry humor.

"Yes. It is difficult to believe we could be so closely related."

"My thoughts precisely."

"Of course, I might improve upon closer acquaintanceship. I am, after all, considered quite irresistible by many young ladies."

The gray eyes once again flashed silver. Luke had no doubt that it was only the presence of Miss Stowe that kept her from tossing one of the lovely figurines at his head.

"Was there something in particular you desired, my lord?"

"I thought we might discuss a mutual acquaintance."

"Mutual acquaintance?"

"Our delightful friend Toby."

"Oh." Her irritation faded as she cast a covert glance at the lady in the corner. "Would you care for tea, my lord?"

"Excellent notion."

"Miss Stowe, may I impose upon you to see if Cook has any fresh scones?"

"Certainly." The elder woman instantly rose, but there was a shrewd glint in her dark eyes. "I shall be gone but a moment."

With her warning delivered, Miss Stowe quietly left the room, careful to leave the door open. Miss Stanholte barely waited until they were alone before she turned back toward him.

"What has occurred?"

Luke smiled in a lazy fashion, fully intending to enjoy their brief moment of privacy to the utmost.

"First, tell me how you are adjusting to your move."

She frowned with impatience. "Well enough."

"Is there anything you require?"

Most ladies of his acquaintance would have responded with an arch laugh and a subtle invitation. Miss Stanholte merely shook her head.

"If there is, I am perfectly capable of acquiring it on my own."

"Naturally," Luke retorted in dry tones. "At least allow me to tell you how extraordinarily beautiful you appear. As much as I regret the loss of the enticing Lady Greer, I far prefer the innocent charms of Miss Stanholte."

For a fleeting moment, a charming confusion rippled over her delicate features; then she was hastily thinning her lips.

"I have no need for your flattery, sir."

"I also noted you have managed to ensnare both Lord Westwood and Mr. Talvert."

"Do not be absurd. They were simply being kind."

"That I very much doubt. Neither one of them could take their gazes off you." Luke was surprised by the sharp edge to his tone.

Miss Stanholte's frown merely deepened. "Do you have information regarding Toby or not?"

Sensing he had pressed the lady as far as he dared, Luke gave a shrug.

"Biddles and I managed to follow him to the theater."

"Did he confess why he tried to kidnap me?"

"We didn't have the opportunity to question him."

"Why not?"

Luke lifted a slender hand. "He was already engaged."

"So you have discovered nothing?" she accused in exasperation.

"Actually, I have discovered some very intriguing information."

"What is it?"

He glanced pointedly at the open door. "We can hardly discuss such a subject with Miss Stowe about to reappear at any moment."

"Then we shall go to the library."

"I believe Miss Stowe intends to take her

168

duties as a chaperon quite to heart. She will only follow us."

"Lord Mumford —"

"No, I fear our only excuse for privacy is a respectable drive through the park," he overrode her angry retort. "I shall call for you tomorrow afternoon."

Even as the words left Luke's mouth, he wondered at his strange behavior. Since when had the Earl of Mumford been reduced to blatant blackmail to induce a young lady to receive his attentions?

Since a blond-haired, dove-eyed minx had tumbled into his life, he silently acknowledged, smiling at his own folly.

Opening her mouth to refuse his expert manipulations, Miss Stanholte was caught short as Miss Stowe swept determinedly back into the room carrying a silver tray.

"Here we are, Miss Cassandra. Straight from the oven."

Nine

"If you will note the attention to detail, Miss Stanholte, you will see the hand of a master. Such exquisite color and light."

Obediently studying the framed painting, Cassie stifled a traitorous yawn. It was not that she did not appreciate the wondrous collection of Van Dykes and Rubens that lined the vast gallery. She possessed a great love for art and greatly envied Lady Pembroke. But while she could imagine nothing more pleasurable than spending an evening, or even several evenings, gazing upon the masterpieces, she found the monotone lecture by Lord Westwood unbearably tedious.

For the better part of an hour Cassie had endured the painfully obvious comments and patronizing manner that marked the young gentleman as a first-rate bore. Indeed, she had barely crossed the threshold when he had pounced upon her and all but hauled her up the stairs to the gallery. Now she found it decidedly difficult to conjure a means of ridding herself of his possessive presence.

"Yes, quite lovely," she murmured, desperately glancing toward the staircase in the hope of relief.

What she found instead was the tall, sinfully handsome Lord Mumford leaning with indolent ease against the carved walnut balustrade. She felt her heart falter as she encountered the amused blue gaze. Really, he was the most disgraceful rogue.

So why then did her knees feel weak and her hands sweaty?

Easily holding her wide gaze, Lord Mumford slowly straightened and strolled across the French Savonnerie carpet. Cassie stiffened, wondering how long he had been watching her.

Unaware of her distraction Lord Westwood continued his droning lecture. "Of course, the Flemish artists are renowned for their —"

"Ah, there you are, Westwood," Luke interrupted as he halted next to Cassie.

The younger man's features settled in petulant lines as he regarded the elegant gentleman attired in a black fitted coat and silver gray waistcoat.

"Mumford."

"Lady Pembroke is requesting your presence in the front salon."

Lord Westwood frowned. "Please inform Lady Pembroke that I will be with her directly."

"I believe she wishes to discuss the placement of the candelabra you requested for your reading."

There was nothing in his bland tone or expression to imply his amusement over the evening's entertainment, but Lord Westwood instinctively stiffened.

"Very well." He turned to Cassie. "Miss Stanholte, will you accompany me?"

Cassie was in a decided quandary. She sternly assured herself that she could not possibly desire to spend a moment alone with Lord Mumford. But she could not deny a reprehensible desire to be free of Lord Westwood.

It was Lord Mumford who took command of the situation.

"Really, Westwood, it is devilish bad *ton* to monopolize poor Miss Stanholte," he drawled. "Besides, I have promised to show her Aunt Sophia's watercolors."

Lord Westwood opened his mouth to argue; then realizing that he would only appear a fool by squabbling with the older man in public, he offered Cassie a stiff bow.

"I shall return in a moment, my dear."

Cassie watched the younger gentleman as he moved toward the staircase before she turned to face Lord Mumford with her familiar exasperation.

"Must you order everyone about, my lord?"

Thoroughly unrepentant, Luke firmly tucked her arm beneath his own and began leading her further along the gallery.

"Be honest, Miss Stanholte. I just performed a most timely service for you."

Well aware that more than one gaze was trained in their direction, Cassie had little choice but to follow his lead.

"I cannot think how depriving me of a charming companion is providing me with a service."

"Charming?" Luke gave a low chuckle. "Is that why your eyes were glazed over and you were so desperately attempting to stifle a yawn?"

A sudden, wholly renegade flare of humor melted her annoyance. This gentleman knew her far too well. Attempting to quash the unworthy sentiment, Cassie conjured a prim expression.

"Lord Westwood is a very agreeable gentleman."

"He is also an insufferable bore."

"My lord —"

"Now, now, Miss Stanholte," he interrupted with a glint in the blue eyes. "I believe we should call a cease-fire. We would not wish to cause undue gossip." He neatly

pulled her to a halt in front of a pastel water-
color in a shallow alcove. "What do you
think of my aunt's gathering?"

She paused, then allowed a rueful smile to
curve her mouth. Perhaps he was right. A
cease-fire would make a pleasant change.

"It is quite . . . elegant," she at last responded. "I feel quite a dowd among so
many beautiful ladies."

The blue eyes darkened. "You must know
that you are by far the most lovely lady
present."

A most absurd flutter of confusion
brought a flush to her cheeks. With a silent
chastisement of her missish behavior, she
swiftly turned toward the painting of the
Grand Canal.

"Are these the watercolors you wished to
show me?"

With a smooth motion Luke moved to
lean against the paneling, his expression
strangely intent.

"Tell me of your home in Devonshire,"
he abruptly commanded.

She glanced at him in surprise. "What do
you wish to know?"

"You have risked your reputation, even
your life, to save your estate. It obviously
means a great deal to you."

A great deal? Cassie gave a slow shake of

her head. It was everything.

"It was all I had left after my parents died," she said, the very simplicity of her words revealing the stark sense of loss that still haunted her.

"Still, it must be a great deal of responsibility."

She shrugged. "It is a responsibility that I enjoy. What could be more satisfying than watching the seasons turn or seeing the tenants bring in the harvest?" Her expression unknowingly softened as she thought of the rolling meadows of her estate. "Every day is like a new beginning."

He appeared oddly captivated by her obvious sincerity. "And you do not find it tedious?"

Uncertain why he should be interested in her attachment to Stanholte Estate, Cassie replied with blunt honesty.

"How could I? There is the house to manage, the accounts to keep, the repairs on the farms, and of course the tenants to see to. And my horses . . ." Abruptly realizing she was revealing far more of herself than she intended, Cassie came to a self-conscious halt. "I am sorry. You cannot be interested."

"But I am," he firmly insisted, his gaze locked on her wide eyes as if he were delving into her heart. "I only wish I possessed your obvious devotion to my own estate. You will be shocked to know that I have quite often considered it a burden rather than a blessing."

Absurdly, Cassie felt a pang of sympathy for the exasperating lord, despite the fact he must be the most envied gentleman in England. She was well aware she had been fortunate to be raised by parents who trained her to respect and care for the land. Lord Mumford, in contrast, had been forced to use his wits and swift intelligence to ensure his livelihood. It was little wonder he found the notion of a demanding estate rather dull. Still, he appeared sincere in his regret that he did not possess her dedication.

"Perhaps that is because you were not raised on the estate," she suggested in soft tones. "In time you will discover that it has become a part of you."

His slow smile seemed to steal her very breath. "I certainly hope you are correct, Miss Stanholte. Despite my sometimes flippant manner, I should like to be a good earl."

Quite impulsively she laid a hand upon his arm. "Then I am sure you will be."

His hand swiftly rose to cover hers with delicious warmth.

"Miss Stanholte —"

Oblivious to all but each other, neither Cassie nor Lord Mumford noted the dark-haired beauty who determinedly marched in their direction. It was only when the lady boldly latched on to Lord Mumford's arm, effectively knocking Cassie aside, that they realized their brief moment of privacy was at an end.

"Lord Mumford, what a delight," the woman purred, overtly ignoring the slender lady at his side.

Stifling an unexplainable stab of disappointment, Cassie regarded the intruder with a narrowed gaze.

She was certainly beautiful, Cassie reluctantly acknowledged. Attired in a deep burgundy gown trimmed with Brussels lace, she possessed a sophistication that Cassie could only envy. Her own gown was a more modest satin of pale green, trimmed with velvet ribbons and seed pearls.

Of course, a spiteful voice whispered in the back of her mind, the cut of the older lady's gown would have made the most daring courtesan proud. A wrong move or a sudden sneeze might very well reveal the full bounty of her charms.

Appearing surprisingly immune to the lovely vision clinging to his arm, Lord

Mumford peered down his nose in a bored manner.

"Lady Bross. May I introduce Miss Stanholte?"

Lady Bross made no effort to acknowledge the introduction and instead pressed herself even closer to the large male form.

Shameless jade, Cassie seethed.

"I missed you at Lady Montelle's ball," she said, batting her long lashes.

"Did you?"

"I was quite certain you would attend."

Lord Mumford shrugged. "I have been rather occupied."

"It was a dreadful squeeze, of course. Still, I had hoped we might have the occasion to further our acquaintance." She coyly lowered her gaze. "We had such a lovely time at the Stanford hunting party."

Lord Mumford's smile was without humor. "Oh, did you attend? I had quite forgotten."

Cassie smothered a gasp at the direct cut, but Lady Bross was clearly made of sterner stuff. Smoothing the lines of anger, she gave an arch laugh.

"What a tease you are, my lord. You could not have forgotten our strolls through the garden nor our morning rides."

"My memory is unfortunately not what it

once was," Luke drawled.

Clearly immune to insult, Lady Bross relentlessly plunged on.

"Will you be traveling with the prince to Brighton this year?"

"I possess a decided aversion to the sea, Lady Bross." Plucking the clinging hand from his arm, Lord Mumford performed a formal bow. "Please excuse us."

Ignoring the unflattering color that crawled beneath the woman's pale skin, Luke turned to clasp Cassie's elbow and led her firmly away. Neither spoke as he steered her toward the staircase. For some reason, Cassie was decidedly annoyed with the forward Lady Bross. At last she turned her gaze to study his rigid profile.

"She is quite . . . persistent. Are all ladies of fashion so forward?"

His stern countenance softened into the more familiar amusement at her tart tone. Shifting his head, he met her disapproving gaze.

"You cannot credit what I am forced to endure, Miss Stanholte," he lightly teased. "There is no end to the female wiles. Indeed, during the house party Lady Bross mentioned I was forced to bolt my bedchamber door each night simply to protect my virtue."

With an effort, she smothered her absurd annoyance. What did she care if every female in London tossed herself at his feet?

"Of course, the Irresistible Earl," she retorted in dry tones.

"Irresistible indeed. I have even had desperate maidens go so far as to throw themselves beneath my carriage."

Her lips quivered. "They must be desperate indeed."

The astonishing blue gaze lingered on her full mouth. "Desperate and quite uncommonly beautiful."

Once again she felt that oddly breathless tingle of excitement. But as before, the intimate moment was swiftly interrupted. On this occasion, it was by a uniformed footman who carried a folded note in his hand.

"Lord Mumford, this was delivered for you."

"Thank you."

With a frown, Luke accepted the note, flicking it open and swiftly reading the few sentences. His brows rose before he was lifting his head to meet her curious gaze.

"I fear I must take my leave."

Cassie was startled by the abrupt announcement. She completely forgot she should be relieved that he would not be around to bother her.

"But Lord Westwood's poetry . . ."

He flashed her a boyish grin. "Yes, I am quite desolate to be denied such a wondrous treat, but duty calls."

Her expression became suspicious. "Has something occurred?"

"I shall explain all tomorrow."

So there was something afoot.

"Lord Mumford."

"Yes?"

"Take me with you," she pleaded softly.

"Do not be a goose," he chided in firm tones. "Not only would both of our reputations be in shreds, but I have no intention of allowing you to place yourself in any further danger."

Her lips thinned. "You have no right —"

With familiar ease, he lifted her fingers to his mouth.

"Until tomorrow."

Unwilling to create a scene, Cassie could only watch as the elegant form moved to the sweeping staircase. Then she sighed in frustration.

It was all utterly unfair, she decided, completely ignoring the horrible frights she had received at the hands of Toby. Not only had Lord Mumford simply disappeared, but he had trapped her into a dreary evening of

Lord Westwood's poetry. At the very least, he should have offered to take her along.

It was one more sin to add to a very long list.

Tossing the reins of his mount to the waiting servant, Luke regarded the entrance of the discreet gaming club with a hint of puzzlement.

The note had commanded him to make an appearance at the club as swiftly as possible. It had not been signed, but the small x at the bottom was Biddles's personal code. Luke could only presume his friend had managed to unearth new information regarding Miss Stanholte.

A reluctant smile tugged at his firm mouth as he entered the narrow stairs to the gaming rooms. It had been a decided wrench to leave Miss Stanholte's side. Not even the hideous spectacle of Lord Westwood's poetry had dulled the pleasure of being in her company.

How brilliantly her eyes had gleamed when she had spoken of her home. He had found himself almost envious. Could a mere gentleman ever stir such devotion in her remote heart?

It was a thought he quickly suppressed.

To be fascinated by a young maiden's

eyes was a blatant warning to a confirmed bachelor. He would be a fool not to flee before it was too late.

With an unconscious shrug, Luke turned his attention to the smoke-filled room. Several tables were scattered throughout the room, with a handful of gentlemen seated at each one. Further on, a sideboard of refreshments was situated along one wall, as well as an open door that led to an even more smoke-filled room.

Luke raised his quizzing glass to survey the crowd, unsurprised to discover a number of hardened gamesters as well as a fair sprinkling of fresh-faced bucks too naive to realize their danger.

He smiled with rueful regret as a servant approached him.

"Lord Mumford, welcome," he murmured.

"Is Lord Bidwell within?"

"Yes, my lord. This way."

Crossing the tiled floor, the servant led him through the far door and toward a small table nearly hidden in the shadows. Taking the seat offered, Luke regarded the slender gentleman attired in a bright yellow coat.

"Dashing as always, Biddles."

"Ah, Mumford, how kind of you to join me so swiftly." Lord Bidwell waved the hovering servant away with a languid hand.

"I presume it is important?"

"Do you recognize the gentlemen at the far table?"

Shifting so that he could covertly study the four gentlemen engaged in a heated game of vingt-et-un, Luke gave a slow nod.

"Trandel, Halvern, Lutty and" — his gaze narrowed at a plump, red-headed gentleman attired in a gaudy striped coat — "a mushroom upstart with a loathsome taste in coats."

Biddles took a sip of brandy. "An upstart who is referred to as Herbie."

"Ah . . ." Luke's interest instantly sharpened.

"If he is like most gentlemen, he will spend another hour drinking too heavily and losing the larger share of his quarterly allowance. Then he will seek the comfort of his mistress's arms."

Luke settled himself more comfortably in the wing chair.

"The elusive Nell."

"Precisely."

"I once again bow to your skill." Luke reached forward to pour himself a healthy measure of brandy and lifted the crystal glass in a silent tribute. "How did you discover he would be here?"

Biddles accepted his tribute with a roguish grin. "Lutty makes an effort to keep a close watch on the greenhorns with a bit of the ready to lay on a wager. He recalled winning a tidy sum from a gent by the name of Herbie several weeks ago." He nodded his head in the direction of the table. "I requested he invite him back for another fleecing. Lutty was only too pleased to comply."

"Now we can only hope that this is the Herbie we search for."

Stretching out his long legs, Luke prepared for a long wait. The evening was still young, and having watched Lutty in action, Luke was aware he used exquisite care not to startle his quarry into flight. It often took hours before the hapless victim realized the extent of his losses.

Luke, however, underestimated Herbie's stunning lack of skill with cards, as well as his ability to be goaded into placing a ludicrous wager on a hopeless cause. Within a remarkably short time Herbie was signing a large stack of notes and staggering to his feet.

Luke and Biddles remained seated until the gentleman had lurched out of the room. Then bowing toward the smug Lutty, they carefully followed behind.

With casual ease they tracked the unsteady Herbie down the stairs and into the street. They waited in the shadows until he had retrieved his mount and urged him away from the club. Then they gathered their own horses and plodded over the cobblestones at a measured pace. Although Herbie had appeared sunk in shocked misery over his disastrous evening, Luke wanted to take no chances.

They traveled through several neighborhoods before at last halting at a small establishment. Luke and Biddles remained carefully hidden behind a shabbily trimmed hedge as Herbie moved up the path and pounded on the door. It took but a moment for a housekeeper to pull open the door.

"Welcome, sir. I shall inform Miss Maggert you have arrived."

Luke and Biddles exchanged a glance at the familiar name. This was the actress they had wanted.

"Tell her not to keep me waiting," Herbie growled as he entered and slammed the door behind him.

On the point of dismounting to find a more favorable view of the house, Luke was halted as a side door opened to reveal a young lady with dark curls and a tall gentleman with a familiar scar down one cheek.

Luke stiffened as he heard Biddles give a low hiss.

He longed to charge through the hedge and choke a confession from the evil man. Or perhaps beat it out of him. It was only the knowledge that, as satisfying as it might be to wrap his hands about the villain's neck, it would not cure Miss Stanholte's troubles that kept him huddled in secret as Nell glanced nervously about her.

"You must go," she whispered as she wrapped a silk robe closer around her full body.

"Do not play me for a fool, Nell," he rasped as he glared down at her white face.

"I have told you I do not know why Miss Stanholte should want me."

"I think you do."

"No, please —"

Her words were cut off as a riding crop was pressed to her throat.

"Have you contacted her?" the gentleman demanded.

Her harsh breathing filled the night air. "No."

"But you have contacted Liza."

"I only warned her to be careful," she pleaded.

The man laughed with cold cruelty. "It is you that should be careful, Nell. I will not tolerate any interference with my plans."

"You don't frighten me," the actress breathed with surprising courage.

"Then you are a fool." With lightning speed, the riding crop was replaced by a gloved hand that curved around her throat. "I could break you as easily as a twig."

Both Luke and Biddles prepared to leap forward. They could not stand aside and watch the madman abuse the helpless actress.

"Let me go," Nell gasped, her eyes wide with fright.

"Heed my warning, Nell." As swiftly as he had attacked, the gentleman stepped back. "It would be a shocking waste for such a lovely wench to be found floating in the Thames."

Giving a choked cry, Nell turned and rushed back into the house. At the same moment, the man sprinted toward the back of the house and disappeared.

Luke instinctively prepared to follow when common sense warned it would be futile. The streets were far too deserted not to alert a man on his guard that he was being followed. Once again Luke would be forced to bide his time. But at least they had discovered Nell.

Turning, he discovered Biddles calmly returning his gun to his pocket.

"That gentleman would be greatly improved with a sword lodged through his bowels," he murmured.

"My thoughts as well." Luke grimaced. "Come. There is little more we can do tonight."

Ten

It was a lovely afternoon. One of those rare spring days when the sky appeared a translucent blue and the air smelled of daffodils.

Not that Miss Stanholte took much notice of the beauty surrounding her. Seated next to Lord Mumford in the open carriage, she silently seethed at the endless flirtatious glances and bold attempts to claim the attention of the gentleman at her side.

Really, she thought as they threaded their way through the crowded park, one would think Lord Mumford was the only gentleman in all of London. They could not pass a carriage without some woman or other calling his name and pleading for a moment of his time.

She refused to admit that he was indeed the most splendidly handsome man about. Attired in a dark blue coat and leather breeches, he easily cast the less notable gentlemen in the shade. She only knew that she was becoming increasingly annoyed at being plagued by the bevy of eager females.

Sensing her escort's curious regard,

Cassie reluctantly turned to meet the narrowed blue gaze.

"Do you intend to sulk the entire afternoon?" he at last inquired with a quirk of his lips.

She felt heat fill her face as she realized he was well aware of her annoyance. For goodness sakes, he would begin to think she was jealous if she were not careful.

"I am not sulking," she sternly denied.

He chuckled at her patent lie. "Very well. Tell me, did you enjoy Lord Westwood's poetry?"

He was clearly in a mood to tease, and she determinedly suppressed a grimace. The poetry had been quite ghastly. For hours Lord Westwood had droned on about the colors of a sunset and the taste of a freshly caught salmon. And to make matters worse, he had composed several long verses dedicated to her and her supposed beauty. Cassie had been sunk in mortification as every eye had turned in her direction.

Her only consolation had been that Lord Mumford had not been there to witness her embarrassment. Now she sighed in resignation. Trust the wretched man to have somehow discovered her discomfiting ordeal.

"It was quite . . . delightful," she forced

herself to say. "He is a most accomplished gentleman."

His smile only widened. "Yes, indeed. My aunt informs me that he composed an ode to you. I believe he compared you to a dove."

A hint of mockery in his tone made her arch a haughty brow.

"Do you find that amusing, my lord?"

"I find it ludicrous," he corrected without hesitation, his gaze sweeping over her features to linger on the militant line of her full lips. "Any lady less like a dove I have yet to encounter."

"You no doubt would have preferred that he likened me to a shrew?"

"You certainly possess your shrewish moments, but I prefer a swan," he startled her by admitting in low tones. "Graceful, proud and independent."

A sudden shyness had her ducking her head in an unconsciously coy manner. Just when she thought she was beginning to know Lord Mumford, he managed to catch her off guard.

"As you said, it was all quite ludicrous," she muttered.

For a moment he was silent as he studied her fragile profile. Then, as they turned to a less crowded part of the park, he leaned forward.

"I am curious, Miss Stanholte. Is there a gentleman in Devonshire you intend to marry?"

She stiffened at his intimate questioning. She was unaccustomed to discussing her life or emotions with anyone, let alone a disturbingly attractive gentleman.

"Sir —"

"Yes, I know, I am impertinent." He negligently waved aside his one of many faults. "Is there?"

"No."

His gaze narrowed in a probing manner. "Perhaps you prefer to capture a London gentleman?"

He sounded almost as if he were accusing her, and Cassie bristled with indignation.

"I have no wish to capture any gentleman," she retorted in sharp tones. "My only desire is to return to my estate and live there in peace."

Strangely, this did not appear to satisfy him any more than the suspicion that she was stalking through London in search of gullible prey. Although the reason why he should be so interested in her marital state eluded her.

"Alone?"

"Certainly." She eyed him squarely. "You reside on your own."

He gave a small shrug. "For now."

His response startled her, and she found herself frowning with disbelief. "Do you intend to wed?"

He appeared to carefully contemplate his answer, and Cassie discovered herself oddly holding her breath.

"It is not something I have given a great deal of thought until now," he admitted, his expression thoughtful. "I suppose in due time I shall have need of an heir."

Her breath rushed out at his words, almost as if she were relieved.

"A marriage of convenience."

"Oh, no," he swiftly denied. "I shall demand more than mere convenience from my marriage."

Her gaze unknowingly narrowed. "And what is that?"

"Companionship, joy . . ." His voice lowered to a husky note. "Love."

A wholly unexpected stab of pain lanced through her heart. It was certainly none of her concern if he wished to fall in love a dozen times a day. That didn't, however, prevent her from envisioning him locked in the embrace of an exquisite beauty.

In an effort to hide her absurd reaction, she gave a forced laugh.

"Love?"

With a deliberate motion, he reached out to brush a small leaf that had fallen onto her bare shoulder. A blaze of heat rushed through her body at the brief touch.

"Just because I do not go about spouting ghastly poetry does not signify I have no heart."

"I thought you considered debutantes a fate worse than the hangman's noose." Her voice was annoyingly uneven.

"Only those debutantes who regard me as the prize fox in their particular hunt," he retorted, closely watching the color rise and fade in her cheeks. "I should like to think that someday I shall be as fortunate as my parents in their marriage." His dark head tilted to one side. "Did your parents marry for convenience?"

As always, Cassie discovered herself retreating from the painful memories of her parents. Even after all this time, she found it difficult to think of the past.

How did anyone ever become accustomed to such a loss? The shock of their deaths had left her alone and all too aware of how easily happiness could be snatched away.

"No," she at last breathed, her expression unconsciously vulnerable. "My mother was the youngest daughter of the local vicar and not at all suitable for my father's family.

They expected him to follow in the Stanholte tradition and marry an heiress. Eventually they eloped."

It was a fairy-tale story that Cassie had demanded be told time and time again: her beautiful mother stealing the heart of the local lord, and he in turn romantically sweeping her into a secret wedding. Quite enchanting for a young, susceptible girl.

"And they were happy?" he asked softly.

"Very happy."

The fine gray eyes darkened as she recalled the laughter and fun that had once filled the estate. She had never thought it would end.

But it did, and all she had was the estate. Now even that was being threatened.

A gentle hand softly brushed her cheek.

"I have made you sad," Lord Mumford murmured with genuine regret.

"No . . ." She gave a small shake of her head, oddly disappointed when the comforting fingers moved away. "I simply miss them."

"And yet you choose to be alone," he pointed out.

Drawing in a deep breath, Cassie attempted to regain her composure. The past was gone. It was the future that concerned her now.

"I believe we came here to discuss what you have discovered?" she reminded him in stiff tones.

As if sensing her withdrawal, Lord Mumford smiled in a rueful manner and signaled to his groom to pull aside.

"Very well. Shall we take a stroll?" Waiting until the carriage came to a halt, he stepped down and turned to lift her out and gently place her on the path. The scent of warm male skin and tangy cologne made her head spin. It did nothing to help when he firmly placed her hand on his arm and began leading her through the sun-dappled park. They walked in silence until they were assured no one could overhear their conversation; then he gazed down at her face with a somber expression. "Do you know a tall, dark gentleman with a scar on his right cheek?"

She frowned in confusion. "Why?"

"Biddles and I tracked Toby to his favorite theater, and he was conversing with the rather dastardly gentleman."

A faint, annoyingly elusive memory brushed the edges of her mind. A scar. She remembered . . . a tall man standing in her father's library. There had been a loud argument, all the more startling because her father never raised his voice. She had peeked through an open window and seen the man holding his cheek as if he had been struck.

"There is something," she said, straining to capture the fuzzy image. "A man with a bleeding cheek . . . oh, I cannot remember."

"Was he in Devonshire?"

"Yes, he was in our home," she confirmed, her brow furrowed. "Do you think he might know Liza or Nell?"

He gave a decisive nod of his head. "I am certain of it. I am also certain that he is the villain who is determined to steal your estate."

Her steps faltered as she gazed up at him in disbelief.

"Why did you not capture him?" she demanded.

His brows rose in mild protest. "Always presuming I would not be killed in such an absurd endeavor, what would you have me do with him?"

Was he being deliberately thick-skulled?

"Take him to the magistrate and reveal what you have learned."

"Unfortunately I cannot simply accuse a man to get him locked in Newgate. I must have some proof of his crime."

Her frown only deepened. She wanted to argue, but even she had to realize he was correct. Without some evidence of the man's connection to Lady Stanholte, they could do nothing.

"Then we are no further than we were before," she said, her frustration at the seemingly insurmountable difficulties bubbling to the fore. "I should have remained where I was. At least then I might have a hope of discovering Nell."

Without warning, Lord Mumford came to a halt, and taking hold of her hands, pulled her to face him. Lifting her head, she encountered his simmering blue gaze.

"Can you not trust me?" he demanded in persuasive tones.

They were so close she could feel the heat from his body and see the darkening of his beard beneath smooth skin. For a crazed moment she was tempted to lift her hand and run her fingers along the strong line of his jaw.

With a wrench, she pulled her thoughts from the unsettling image.

"It is . . . difficult," she acknowledged with a shiver. "I am unaccustomed to depending upon anyone but myself."

He looked deep into her eyes, as if he could see into the pain that had held her prisoner since her parents' deaths.

"I will not fail you," he promised as he

gently squeezed her fingers.

Lost in the velvet blue eyes, Cassie might have remained gaping into his countenance for hours if they had not been interrupted by a gentleman attired in a fitted coat and glossed boots. Hearing the approaching footsteps, Cassie turned to regard the pleasant-featured gentleman with a thatch of blond curls.

"Miss Stanholte." He bowed, his smile quite charming. "I had hoped I might see you today." As an obvious afterthought, he nodded toward her companion. "Lord Mumford."

Luke's features hardened with displeasure. "Champford."

His duty done, the young nobleman returned his attention to Cassie.

"Do you attend the theater this evening?"

Telling herself that she was relieved by the intrusion, Cassie managed a smile.

"Yes, indeed."

"Then I shall make certain to attend as well," Lord Champford promised, his gaze sweeping over her elegant muslin gown. "May I say you are looking remarkably lovely today? Quite as beautiful as spring itself."

Hearing Lord Mumford's exasperated grunt at the flowery compliment, Cassie deliberately fluttered her long lashes. After enduring the sickening number of females tossing themselves before Lord Mumford, it seemed only fair that she have at least one admirer.

"Thank you, my lord," she simpered in the manner of the other debutantes. "I was particularly doubtful about this shade of violet."

Lord Champford appeared gratifyingly enchanted. "It is absolutely splendid. Quite perfect."

She lowered her gaze. "You are too kind."

"It is so refreshing to meet a maiden who appreciates the charm of modesty," he insisted in fervent tones. "So many young ladies are shockingly lacking in propriety these days, do you not agree?"

The irony was not lost on Lord Mumford, who gave a sudden laugh.

"Ah, yes, Miss Stanholte is a great believer in propriety," he taunted as her face filled with heat. Then, clearly having enough of the nauseating flirtation, he took Cassie's arm firmly in his grip. "Now I fear you will have to excuse us."

Lord Champford hastily grabbed Cassie's hand to lift it to his lips.

"Perhaps I may call on you tomorrow?"

Conscious of Luke's narrowed gaze,

Cassie gave an encouraging nod.

"But of course."

With a sudden tug, Luke turned her away and began marching her back toward the waiting carriage. Strangely, Cassie quite enjoyed the hint of annoyance that marred his noble features.

"I must congratulate you, Miss Stanholte," he said, at last breaking the silence. "Lord Champford is considered one of the finest catches in the marriage mart."

She gave a vague shrug. "He is very charming."

"He is also extremely wealthy and in line to become the fifth Earl of Wilthaven."

Lifting her head, she directly met his probing gaze. "What a pity that I did not think to twist my ankle or toss myself beneath his carriage."

Without warning, the irritation faded from his countenance and he laughed with rich appreciation of her tart reply.

"Minx," he softly chided, his hand reaching up to stroke the full curve of her bottom lip. "Come along, or I shall forget that a gentleman does not kiss a maiden in full view of a public park."

Cassie experienced a sharp, nearly painful desire that he would forget propriety and gather her into his arms. As difficult as it was to admit, she could not deny she longed to once again experience the sweet pleasure of his kiss.

The treacherous weakness held her silent as Luke handed her into the carriage and they turned to make their way back to her town house.

Lord Mumford chatted easily on the return trip, seemingly unaware of her air of distraction. It was only when he escorted her to the door and placed a lingering kiss on her slender fingers that she was at last roused from her brooding thoughts.

"Thank you for a most delightful afternoon, Miss Stanholte," he murmured.

Waiting for him to demand that she join him for another ride the following day, she was disconcerted when he simply turned and walked back to the waiting carriage.

Would she ever understand the unsettling gentleman?

Shortly arriving at his own town house, Luke discovered himself whistling softly as he vaulted out of the carriage and headed up the steps to the open door. What a perfectly delightful afternoon, he thought with a small grin. Who would have suspected that a simple drive with a young lady could be so satisfying?

Entering the foyer of the lavish house, Luke allowed his butler to relieve him of his hat and gloves.

"Lord Bidwell is waiting in the library, my lord," the elderly servant informed Luke as he peered in an oval mirror to adjust his cravat.

"Thank you, Gibson."

Rather curious at the unexpected visit, Luke made his way down the hallway to enter the private library. Although not a large room, it managed to contain an astonishing number of leather-bound books as well as a large Sheraton writing desk. Two comfortable wing chairs faced the black marble chimneypiece, and Luke was unsurprised to discover Biddles sprawled in one with a large glass of brandy and a cigar.

"I see that Gibson has seen to your comfort," Luke drawled as he crossed the patterned carpet to lean against the desk.

"Devilish fine chap," Biddles commended. "Bit of a tartar about sharing your private stash of brandy, however."

Luke deliberately regarded the fine crystal decanter set on a table close to the chair.

"I note you managed to corrupt his better judgment."

Biddles smiled with smug satisfaction. "I

do have my little ways."

Luke couldn't prevent a small chuckle. He was quite familiar with this gentleman's devious ways.

"So what brings you to my home, besides your appreciation for my cellar?"

Biddles stretched out his legs as he puffed on his cigar.

"I thought you would wish to know that this morning while I was taking a stroll I managed to turn my ankle in quite a nasty manner."

Luke blinked in mild surprise. "How unfortunate. Have you recovered?"

"Yes. Thankfully, a kindhearted actress was just leaving her establishment and rushed to my aid."

Comprehension dawned, and Luke slowly smiled. "I do not suppose this actress possesses the name of Nell?"

Biddles pretended to consider the question before giving a slow smile.

"Why, now that I think upon it, I do believe you are correct. Such a caring soul." He heaved a small sigh. "She insisted that I come inside until my ankle ceased its beastly throbbing."

Luke could only admire his friend's cunning. It had been only a few hours since they had located the actress, and already he had managed to slip into her life.

"Did she happen to mention her friend Liza?"

Biddles lifted his hands in a rueful manner. "I could gather little information in the short time we were together. Perhaps after we meet this evening I will know more."

"This evening?" Luke widened his eyes in disbelief. "What of the faithful Herbie?"

"Miss Maggert is clever enough to realize I am in a position to offer her far more than a mere baron's son," Biddles pointed out in contented tones.

Luke's smile was sardonic. "Naturally."

"And, of course, my charm is quite without comparison."

"Yes, for which I am eternally grateful." With a smooth motion, Luke moved forward to pour himself a measure of brandy. Then he regarded Biddles with a stern gaze. "You will be careful, old chap?"

Biddles squarely met his gaze before giving a firm nod of his head.

"You have my word."

Although he disliked the notion of allowing his friend to place himself in such danger, Luke was well aware he could do little to convince the gentleman to leave the troubles to him. Besides, he needed the clever man's invaluable help if he were to save Miss Stanholte.

Lifting his glass, he sent up a silent prayer. "To success."

A wicked glint suddenly entered Biddles's eyes as he lifted his own glass. "To love, the most daring adventure of all."

Luke hesitated, then slowly smiled in appreciation. "To love."

Eleven

On awakening the next morning, Cassie was startled to discover a summons waiting for her from Lady Pembroke demanding that she call on her as soon as it was convenient. Her heart sank in dismay at the message as she conjured a dozen separate disasters that could have prompted the commanding missive.

Had the lady discovered that Cassie had recently acquired an aunt of dubious character? Or, worse, had she discovered her earlier charade as Lady Greer?

Knowing she could not ignore such a direct request, Cassie attired herself in a jonquil gown and collected Miss Stowe to make the short drive to the elegant town house.

Once there, she was promptly led to a back salon where Lady Pembroke was reading her morning correspondence.

"There you are, my dear." The older woman smiled in satisfaction, waving her hand toward the dragon-clawed sofa.

"Good morning, Lady Pembroke." With a sense of wariness, Cassie moved to perch on the edge of the cushion. Miss Stowe quietly settled beside her. "Did you wish to speak with me?"

"Yes, my dear, I have the most wonderful news."

Cassie's wariness only deepened. "Oh?"

"Lady Fenwell has invited you to her ball."

The expectant expression on Lady Pembroke's face warned Cassie that this was a commendable feat, but for the moment she could only heave a sigh of relief. She hadn't been discovered. At least not yet. Now she could do no more than smile in a feeble manner.

"I see."

Lady Pembroke blinked in obvious surprise. "Do you not realize what this means?"

"Not precisely," Cassie confessed.

Leaning forward, Lady Pembroke regarded her with a shrewd gaze.

"It means, my dear, that you are an undeniable success."

"Oh." With an effort, Cassie kept her smile intact. "I am certain you must be mistaken," she murmured, wondering what the devil was going on.

She was a country Miss without fortune or beauty. She had nothing to commend herself, unless one counted her thorough disregard for courting the favor of the *ton*. It was ludicrous to suggest she had somehow managed to become a success.

Sitting back, Lady Pembroke gave a firm shake of her silver head.

"I am never mistaken about anything of importance," she assured Cassie, absently patting the string of pearls that lay against her deep plum gown. "Lady Fenwell personally requested your presence. Quite an accomplishment for a young debutante."

"Yes, indeed," Miss Stowe was stirred to comment, a rare event indeed. "Lady Fenwell . . . just imagine."

Cassie had no desire to imagine, but with both ladies gazing at her, she gave a faint nod.

"Yes."

There was a small silence as Lady Pembroke subjected her to a probing survey; then the older woman smiled in a worrisome manner.

"Not that I am surprised. You have created a stir since your arrival. Especially among the gentlemen. Every hopeful mama is absolutely green with envy over your having stolen the march on the finest catch of the Season."

Cassie could not halt the sense of shock that jolted through her stiff frame.

"What?"

"Lord Champford, my dear," Lady Pembroke clarified with a faint narrowing of her gaze. "Every beauty in Town has been angling for him for years, but he has refused to show a preference until now."

Cassie felt the color rise and fade in her face.

"Whomever did you think I meant?" Lady Pembroke demanded.

Fool, she silently chided herself. "No one of importance," she breathed.

Still regarding her closely, Lady Pembroke continued, "And, of course, Lord Westwood is determined to make a cake of himself. Not that I would expect you to settle for a mere viscount."

"Lord Westwood has been quite kind."

"He is a silly boy. No, what you need is a man worthy of your obvious spirit," Lady Pembroke announced in firm tones; then that odd smile returned. "Tell me, what do you think of my nephew?"

Feeling as if the clever woman was deliberately attempting to keep her off guard, Cassie struggled to maintain a cool composure.

"He is quite . . . kind."

Lady Pembroke gave a sudden laugh. "He is arrogant, spoiled and far too charming for his own good. Still, he would make a fine husband for a lady clever enough to capture his heart."

Clever? Noddy was more like it, Cassie assured herself. Never had there been a more stubborn, perfectly annoying gentleman. A woman would have to be without sense to deliberately bind herself to him for a lifetime.

Still, she couldn't deny that he did possess the devil's own charm. Why else would she spend night after night recalling the searing pleasure of his kiss?

Lowering her all too revealing gaze, Cassie absently smoothed the muslin skirt.

"I have no interest in acquiring a husband, Lady Pembroke. I am merely in London to see the sights."

"Rubbish. Every woman is in search of a husband. You just have yet to realize it," Lady Pembroke announced in complacent tones, merely smiling when Cassie's gaze abruptly rose in annoyance. "Now, tell me what you will wear to the ball."

"I have not decided if I will attend or not," Cassie retorted in stiff tones.

"But of course you will," Her Ladyship crisply countered, appearing remarkably like her nephew. Cassie could only presume that sheer bloody arrogance was a prevalent trait of the Mumford clan. "It is the most sought after invitation of the Season. Really, my dear, I do not believe you fully realize just how fortunate you have been. There are any number of debutantes that would give their fortunes to be in your position."

As if sensing Cassie's prickly reaction to the admonishment, Miss Stowe offered her a coaxing smile.

"Sophia is quite right. It will be the crowning event of the Season."

"I am certain that it will be delightful —"

"Delightful? Fah," Lady Pembroke interrupted, a suspicious hint of amusement glinting in her eyes. "It will be a horrid squeeze with stale food and watered champagne. The only delight it offers is the opportunity to be seen. Still, only a fool would refuse to attend."

"I am certain my presence would not be missed."

"I assure you that it would. Lady Fenwell is a most conscientious hostess." The older woman smiled in an arch fashion. "And, of course, Lord Champford would be quite distraught if you did not put in an appearance."

Cassie heaved a rueful sigh. She was a woman who was accustomed to doing precisely as she pleased. It was decidedly difficult to encounter anyone with a will as staunch as her own.

"We shall see," she at last conceded.

Clearly satisfied she had won the skirmish, Lady Pembroke turned the conversation to the lovely spring weather and the latest scandal surrounding the prince. Still, Cassie was relieved when the prescribed twenty minutes had elapsed and she was free to make her escape.

Promising to call later in the week, Cassie made her way out of the house and into the waiting carriage. Miss Stowe was close behind her, and soon they were comfortably settled and traveling back through the heavy traffic. They rode in silence for long moments before Miss Stowe slowly turned toward her.

"You mustn't mind Lady Pembroke," she offered in tentative tones. "She has always been quite outspoken."

Cassie smiled with wry humor. Despite her annoyance at being forced to have a companion, she had slowly come to appreciate the older woman's quiet presence and unwavering kindness.

"Yes, I can imagine," she said in dry tones.

"But she means well."

There was another silence; then impulsively Cassie blurted out the question that had haunted her the past several days.

"Do you regret not marrying, Miss Stowe?"

The spinster blinked in surprise but did not hesitate in her reply.

"Very much, but in my situation it was not my own but my brother's decision that I not wed."

"What?"

Miss Stowe smiled at Cassie's startled tone. "The few offers I received were not deemed worthy of my position. My brother was quite adamant in his belief that it was more respectable not to wed than to risk the family name with a questionable connection."

Cassie's already low opinion of Mr. Stowe sank another notch. Really, he was a bully of the worse sort.

"Were you ever in love?"

"Oh, yes." The thin features suddenly softened as Miss Stowe remembered back to the pleasant follies of youth. "I fell in love my first Season with a dashing young gentleman in a uniform."

Curious, Cassie tilted her head to one side. "What was he like?"

"Kind, patient and very, very honorable."

Easily able to imagine a handsome young soldier escorting the once pretty Miss

Stowe, Cassie smiled.

"He sounds quite wonderful."

Surprisingly, Miss Stowe merely grimaced. "Yes, I suppose."

"What is it?"

The older woman gave a self-conscious laugh. "I suppose it is shocking, but in truth, I should have wished that he be less honorable."

Cassie arched her brows in surprise. "What do you mean?"

Miss Stowe ducked her head as if embarrassed to have revealed such an unworthy thought. But beneath Cassie's probing gaze she at last continued.

"When my brother refused to consent to my marriage, I wished to elope," she confessed in low tones. "It did not matter to me that I would be cut off from my family, or even that we would have to survive on his small salary. I only wanted to be his wife."

"But he refused?"

"Yes. He said that it would not be honorable, and that as a gentleman he could not subject me to such a scandal. So he left London, and I never saw him again."

Cassie opened her mouth to insist that the young gentleman had been perfectly right to prevent a scandal. After all, it would have been quite difficult to be cut off from one's family and even Society. He had only been thinking of her. Then she abruptly caught her breath.

No.

There were times when honor was not enough. Hadn't Cassie's own parents chosen love over honor and duty? And hadn't her own determination to save her estate allowed her to behave in a less than commendable manner? Surely, if he had truly cared, this gentleman would have realized that he was condemning Miss Stowe to a life of misery with her brother. A life without love.

What honor was in that?

Without warning, the exquisitely handsome countenance of Lord Mumford rose to her mind. He would not stand aside if he were in love. He would sweep a woman into his arms and never allow her a moment of regret.

Cassie hastily scrubbed the treacherous image from her mind.

"I am so sorry," she murmured softly.

Miss Stowe slowly lifted her head and offered a sad smile.

"Thank you, but it was all a very long time ago."

"Yes, I suppose . . ."

Cassie's doubtful words trailed to a halt as the carriage turned a particularly sharp corner and without warning the small door was jerked open. Miss Stowe screamed as a man leapt into the interior, his face hidden by a thick scarf. Cassie opened her mouth to protest when the man suddenly lifted his hand to reveal a pistol.

Feeling as if she were in some horrible nightmare, Cassie could only watch in horror as the sun glinted off the evil gun pointed directly at her heart. With no space to move and little hope of shoving aside the intruder, there was nothing she could do but wait for the inevitable end.

Squeezing her eyes shut, Cassie listened as Miss Stowe's scream was punctuated by a resounding bang. Then a fierce, scalding pain scraped across her shoulder. She knew she should open her eyes, to fight the mad intruder. But the combination of shock and pain proved too much.

Inwardly she cursed the realization that Lady Stanholte would win after all, as a blanket of darkness clouded her mind in blissful unconsciousness.

It was several hours later when a sharp disturbance intruded into her peace.

"Please, my lord, the doctor has left a

strict command that Miss Stanholte is not to be disturbed," an upstairs maid was desperately saying. "If you would come back in the morning —"

"I have no intention of disturbing Miss Stanholte, but neither do I intend to leave this establishment until I have assured myself that she is still alive. Trust me, it will be easier all around if you simply step aside and allow me to have my way."

Lying on the bed, swimming somewhere between consciousness and engulfing darkness, Cassie listened to the distant exchange with weary humor. If she possessed the strength, she would have warned the unwary maid that arguing with Lord Mumford was a waste of breath. But at the moment, it took all her energy to fight back the burning pain in her shoulder. The maid would simply have to fend for herself.

"The doctor told me the mistress was not to be wakened until the morning."

"I am certain the doctor is a fine gentleman, but I have a vast amount of experience in caring for this impetuous, occasionally insane female and I will not rest easy until I have seen her for myself."

"My lord —"

"Stand aside."

"Here, here." The firm voice of Mrs.

Green intruded in the argument. "What is the trouble?"

"I have come to see Miss Stanholte," Lord Mumford announced in aggressive tones, clearly prepared to have his way. Mary, however, was not easily intimidated. Not even by a six-foot lord with enough arrogance to fill all of England.

"Yes, well, you needn't disturb the entire household," she chided. "That will be all, Emma."

"Yes, mum."

There was a silence as the maid departed, no doubt to spread the rumor that Lord Mumford was forcing his way into the mistress's bedchamber.

"How is she?" Luke at last demanded.

"She'll live, no thanks to that blackguard."

"I want to see her."

"I won't have her disturbed," the housekeeper warned.

With an inward sigh, Cassie at last conceded defeat. It was futile to hope the gentleman would be swayed by the doctor's orders, or even by the sheer indecency of being in her private rooms.

"Oh, for goodness sakes, let him in," she commanded in weak tones. "It is the only means I shall have of gaining peace."

Mary snorted her disapproval as Lord Mumford crossed the room and then boldly perched on the edge of the bed. In the shadowed room, his face appeared remarkably pale and his eyes as dark as night. Grasping her slender fingers, he struggled to conjure his normal composure.

"As charming as ever, I see." His gaze moved to the heavy bandage at her shoulder. "How do you feel?"

She grimaced, well aware that she had been unbelievably fortunate.

"As if I had just been shot," she retorted in wry tones.

Unexpectedly, his features twisted with a flare of sheer fury.

"One day I shall take great pleasure in hanging Toby and his companions." Then with an effort he forced himself to take in a calming breath. "I do not suppose you could identify the man who shot you?"

Cassie gave a sudden shiver. "No. He was wearing a scarf over his face."

"Did he wear a gray coat?"

"I do not recall . . ." Cassie's voice trailed away as a vivid image flashed through her mind. "Wait. Yes. Yes, it was gray."

Luke's eyes abruptly narrowed, his hand tightly grasping her fingers.

"You are not safe here," he growled.

After this morning, she had to agree. Not even her stubborn nature could deny that only sheer luck had saved her life. Someone most desperately wished to be rid of her.

But who?

"And where would I be safe, my lord?" she demanded in weary tones.

"I could find you a house outside of London —"

"And have everyone presume I am your mistress?" she interrupted.

He gave a restless shake of his head, frustration carved into his lean countenance. "The devil take it. At least you would be away from Toby."

"I will only be safe when I have proven Lady Stanholte is a fraud," Cassie pointed out, wincing as the throbbing in her shoulder deepened.

As if sensing she was in no condition for their usual sparring, he gave a rueful smile.

"Then that is what we will do." Slowly he lifted her hand to his mouth, placing a lingering kiss on her fingers before turning her hand over and stroking his lips over her inner wrist. The caress was a poignant reminder of the first occasion he had kissed her in such a fashion, and a pleasant heat stirred in her stomach. "Rest now."

From lowered lids Cassie watched as

Lord Mumford rose to his feet and moved across to where Mrs. Green guarded the door with a forbidding expression. He paused for a moment as he spoke to the housekeeper in a low tone, no doubt issuing commands in his usual arrogant manner. At the moment, however, Cassie was in too much pain to protest.

Instead she gratefully sank back into the waiting darkness.

Twelve

Leaving the bedchamber, Luke determinedly headed for the servants' quarters. The grim expression on his handsome features ensured that even the most seasoned of the staff refrained from attempting to halt his progress.

Luke never noted the nervous maids and pageboys that scurried for safety at his approach. Instead he brooded on the fragile maiden he had left sleeping on the bed upstairs.

When he had first learned of the incident, he had nearly ridden straight for the theater to strangle the pathetic life from Toby. After all, he had been quite certain the vile creature had been responsible for the attack.

But the need to see and touch Miss Stanholte had overwhelmed the lethal impulse. He would deal with Toby before the day was through, but not until he had assured his frantic heart that he had not lost the only woman who could stir his emotions.

Now, the fury that he had been forced to suppress once again coursed through his body. He wanted to know precisely what had occurred, and then he intended to track down the villain responsible.

Entering the kitchen, he spotted a startled footman sipping his tea.

"Fetch the groom," he commanded in abrupt tones.

Without hesitation, the young man scrambled to his feet and hurried out a side door. Within moments, a grizzled man with a ruddy expression and silver hair entered the kitchen and gave an awkward bow. Luke did not have to look closely to tell that the servant had been crying, and he forced back his hasty words of reprimand. The poor man was clearly distraught over what had happened.

"You asked to see me, my lord?" he asked, twisting his hands in a nervous manner.

"I wish to know every detail of what occurred."

The lean face twitched at the memory. "T'ain't much to say. We come around the corner and this cove jumped out of the bushes. He hopped onto the carriage afore we could halt him."

Luke silently pondered the information. The attack had clearly been well prepared. And by someone who had known precisely where to wait for the carriage.

His heart twisted with fear.

"Then what?"

"We heard a shot and the bloke was running away."

"You are certain he was alone?"

"Difficult to say, sir," the groom conceded. "It all happened so fast."

"Yes, I imagine so."

The pale eyes watered as he peered carefully up at Luke. Rather like a faithful hound who had just received a sound beating.

"Miss Stanholte . . . how do she be?"

A sharp pain lanced through Luke as he recalled the slender form lying upon the bed. How tiny and helpless she had appeared. Just as the first time he had seen her, lying upon that damp London street. And now, as then, he had been nearly undone by the fierce need to protect her.

"A simple flesh wound." He set the anxious man's mind at ease. "Thankfully, the assailant appeared to be a shockingly poor shot. Or perhaps he simply lost his nerve."

The sad expression was suddenly hardened with a burst of anger. "I should like to get me hands on the rotter. Better be shot meself rather than know Miss Stanholte be injured."

Luke gave a humorless laugh. "You shall

have to wait your turn," he warned. "I shall have first go at the scoundrel."

"Do you know who he be?"

Luke's hands unconsciously clenched as he allowed his thoughts to turn toward the hatchet-faced Toby.

"Yes, and after this evening he will no longer be troubling Miss Stanholte." He paused, his gaze narrowed with purpose. "But that, unfortunately, does not ensure Miss Stanholte's safety."

As expected, the loyal servant readily squared his shoulders. "What can I do?"

"Good man." Luke smiled, sensing the man would risk his own life before he would allow anything to happen to his young mistress. "I want you to inform me of anyone who appears interested in Miss Stanholte."

The groom nodded. "Aye."

"Somehow the assailant knew where you would be today and where to stand in order to attack," Luke muttered, the thought sending a chill down his spine.

"A pox on his black soul," the man cursed.

Luke fully echoed the dark sentiment. Although he wished more than a pox on him.

"And keep a close watch on the servants," he commanded in stern tones. "If someone within the household is willing to sell information regarding Miss Stanholte, then I want their head on a platter."

"I'll put it there meself," the groom solemnly promised. "Anything else, my lord?"

Luke grimaced as he patted the man on the shoulder. "Pray."

The silver head dipped in agreement. "Aye, I will be doing that."

Unable to withstand the burning need to take action, any action, Luke abruptly turned to make his way through the quiet house and back into the street where his own groom was patiently walking the highstrung grays. At his approach, the servant moved to pull down the step for Luke to climb up to the high perch of the phaeton.

Taking the reins, Luke motioned for the man to join him on the padded seat. He had a great deal to accomplish in a short amount of time and he wanted to ensure that nothing went wrong.

It was several hours later when Luke entered the abandoned cottage well outside of London. Although the house and lands belonged to the Crown, it was often used for covert meetings or to hide individuals who needed to disappear for a time. Now he grimly headed through the vacant rooms to a back chamber that could be bolted from the outside. Standing guard outside the door, Jameson gave his employer a slight nod.

"He has awakened, my lord."

"Thank you, Jameson."

With a swift motion, Luke shoved aside the bolt and opened the heavy door. Inside the cramped chamber, the only furnishings were a straw pallet and a chair. A lone candle burned in the center of the stone floor. Slowly rising to his feet, Toby glared at Luke through blurry eyes.

It had taken Jameson less than an hour to track the narrow-faced gentleman to a disreputable gin house, and only moments to lure him into a back alley where Luke had expertly knocked him unconscious and loaded him into the carriage. Luke had then ordered the groom to go on to the cottage while Luke remained in London to ensure that Ramsel maintained a constant guard on Miss Stanholte. He had also placed a guard on Nell Maggert on the off chance the scar-faced gentleman returned. Only then did he gather his mount and make his way through the early morning light to the remote cottage.

Now he slowly lowered himself into the wooden chair, his expression formidable enough to make Toby press himself against the stone wall.

"Where am I?" the thin man croaked.

Luke narrowed his gaze. "That is the least of your concerns, old chap."

Toby's own gaze nervously darted about the shadowed room, no doubt searching for a means of escape. It took only a moment to realize it was a futile hope.

"What do yer want?"

"Your neck in a noose."

The already pale countenance faded to white. "Blimey."

Luke smiled in a dangerous manner. "But first I need information."

"I ain't tellin' yer nothin'," the prisoner attempted to bluster.

"Oh, I believe you will." With deadly ease Luke reached beneath his caped driving coat to withdraw a loaded pistol. He waited until Toby's dubious nerve failed and he was once again cowering against the wall. "Who hired you to harm Miss Stanholte?"

"I . . . some gent with a scar," he at last stammered.

"That much I know." Luke waved the pistol in a negligent manner. "What is his name?"

"I don't know."

"I am in no humor for lies," Luke warned in harsh tones.

Toby swallowed heavily. "I ain't tellin' no lies."

"I know that you work for this gentleman."

"Yes, but he never say his name," Toby hastily claimed, his gaze warily tracking the gun. "He just come to the theater when he needs me."

Luke was unimpressed. "A clever bloke like you would have no difficulty finding out a mere name. And you would hardly be foolish enough to become employed by a stranger. Better men than you have become acquainted with the hangman's noose for taking coin from a criminal."

A sudden grimace twisted the narrow face as Toby lifted a hand to stroke a fresh scar on his neck.

"I might have poked about a bit, but the gent soon enuf convinced me it be a dangerous habit."

Luke felt a thrust of annoyance. The mystery man was even more clever than he had anticipated. Clearly, the man had suspected Toby was basically a weak man and would swiftly confess all when his own neck was being threatened. He had ensured that his identity would remain a secret.

"You must know something," Luke growled.

Toby nervously licked his lips. "I know that while his clothes be fancy enuf, his mount be rented and his boots borrowed or stolen."

Luke gave the scoundrel credit for being observant, but he was far from appeased. This man had very nearly killed Miss Stanholte. Luke wanted answers and he wanted them now.

He pointed the pistol directly at Toby. "It is hardly unusual for a gentleman to live above his means. I want more."

In the dim light, Luke could see Toby's chest pump in and out as he struggled to breathe.

"I also managed to follow him to a neighborhood not far from the theater afore he give me the slip," he desperately confessed.

"Better," Luke relented. "Did he order you to kill Miss Stanholte today?"

Obviously sensing that a lie would prove more dangerous than the truth, Toby gave a slow nod of his head.

"Yes. He came yesterday and says he needs her out of the way."

Luke trembled with the effort not to react to the chilling words. As much as he might long to horsewhip this cur, he knew that it was far more important that he find out the identity of the scar-faced gentleman. Only

232

then could he ensure that Miss Stanholte was safe.

"How did you know where she would be?"

"I paid the cook's son to tell me where she be goin'."

Luke vaguely recalled an imp who was always darting among the mews. The lad was barely more than twelve and could have little understanding of the danger of passing along such information. Although Luke had every intention of providing the boy with a stern lecture.

Now he regarded Toby with a piercing gaze. "What do you know of Liza?"

"Liza?" Toby shifted with restless unease. "The only Liza I be knowin' worked at the theater until a few months ago. Then she and her brat disappeared."

"Where did she go?"

"She didn't say, and I never asked."

"Did you ever see her with your employer?"

"Naw." Toby's brow furrowed as if he were considering the notion of Liza's connection with the scar-faced gentleman for the first time. "But she used to say how she was marrying a real gent and soon she would have a fine home and plenty of the blunt." Toby abruptly grimaced. " 'Course,

Liza always did lay her bet on a losing horse."

Luke regarded the thin man with a twisted smile. "Much like yourself, eh, Toby?"

Toby's gaze moved back to the pistol in Luke's hand. "What are yer goin' to do with me?"

For a moment Luke allowed the ruffian to fear the worse. He had terrified Miss Stanholte for days and almost stolen her life hours before. He deserved to feel the same fear.

At last consumed with his need to return to Miss Stanholte's side, Luke gave a negligent shrug.

"Eventually you will be handed over to the magistrate. Until then you can remain here."

Toby pushed away from the wall, his expression horrified. "You can't leave me here."

"Would you prefer to return to the theater?" Luke demanded with cold indifference. "No doubt your employer is even now searching for you. He did not impress me as a gentleman who would accept failure gracefully, but perhaps you know him better than I."

A thin hand rose to stroke the scar on his

neck, but Toby was clearly more frightened of the magistrate than his black-hearted employer.

"I can take care of meself."

"Perhaps, but I do not intend to allow you to risk your worthless neck as long as I have need of you." Luke rose to his feet, his countenance without mercy. "Make yourself comfortable, Toby. You are not going anywhere for a while."

"My dear, what an exquisite gown."

Bearing down on Cassie with the determination of an advancing general, Lady Pembroke regarded the simple silk gown in mint green with silver netting with approval. The pure lines added an elegance to Cassie's slight frame. To complement the attire, the golden curls were piled high atop her head with delicate diamond clips. Although Cassie knew the gown suited her fair coloring, she had chosen it for the practical fact that the style of the gown covered the angry scar that still marred the skin of her shoulder.

Realizing that her attempts to remain unnoted amid the vast crowd had failed, Cassie gave a small smile.

"Thank you, Lady Pembroke," she murmured.

"Come." Firmly grasping Cassie's arm, Lady Pembroke steered her behind a large marble pillar. "I must know how are you feeling."

Although it had been over a week since the attack, Cassie still felt her heart falter at the memory. She was not certain she would ever be able to shut her eyes again without seeing the barrel of a pistol pointed at her face.

"Much improved, thank you," she forced herself to say.

"When Luke told me that you had been accosted by a thief in broad daylight, I was horrified, simply horrified."

Although Cassie had wanted to keep the incident a secret, Luke had convinced her that there would be unpleasant gossip unless they came up with some plausible story for the attack. It had been his decision to claim it was a desperate robber that had jumped into the carriage.

"It was a shock."

Lady Pembroke shivered in sympathy. "Just to think, being attacked in a perfectly respectable neighborhood. Are we no longer safe in our own homes? It does not bear thinking of."

"Indeed."

As if sensing Cassie's reluctance to discuss the incident, Lady Pembroke abruptly squared her shoulders.

"But there is no sense in brooding on such unpleasant thoughts. Tonight we are here to enjoy ourselves." She reached out to tap Cassie with her fan. "Indeed, Lord Champford has already arrived."

Cassie diligently smothered a grimace. It was a gentleman such as Lord Champford and Lord Westwood that had induced her into the shadowed corner in the first place.

"Has he?"

Lady Pembroke glared across the room. "Of course, Mrs. Hart pounced upon him the moment he entered. An interfering, self-serving woman. She is determined to marry off that pox-faced chit of hers to a title."

Cassie's own gaze shifted to where the attractive lord was being held prisoner by a large, horse-faced woman in a puce gown.

"I suppose Lord Champford is sought by many hopeful mamas."

"Yes." Lady Pembroke allowed herself a preening smile. "But he has revealed little interest in any but you."

"A wise man," a male voice suddenly drawled. Cassie felt a familiar tingle of excitement inch down her spine as she turned to discover Lord Mumford standing at her side. Attired in a crisply fitted black coat and formal pantaloons, he easily over-shadowed every other gentleman in the room. "What gentleman of good sense could resist the charms of Miss Stanholte?"

"Luke." Lady Pembroke eyed her relative with a knowing smile. "I suppose there is no need to ask why you would choose to make an appearance this evening?"

Cassie felt a blush warm her cheeks, but Luke merely laughed.

"Why, Aunt Sophia, you know that I could not resist such a tempting gathering."

"Fah." Lady Pembroke glanced slyly at the discomfited Cassie. "I fear you will have to excuse me. I promised Miss Stowe that I would introduce her to Lord Elgin. Such an intriguing gentleman."

Without waiting for a response, Lady Pembroke swept around the pillar and swiftly became lost in the crowd. Oddly, Cassie felt extraordinarily shy to be left with Lord Mumford. Over the past week he had become a familiar visitor to her town house, often sitting for hours to read a book or play at cards. She had come to depend upon his pleasurable companionship, quite often for-getting that she was supposed to resent his interfering presence. Indeed, she had dis-covered herself anxiously awaiting his arrival, as if she actually enjoyed his companionship.

And it was that realization that had made her suddenly uneasy.

"Aunt Sophia has never been overly subtle," Lord Mumford remarked in dry tones. "Still, I commend her efforts. It is a rare opportunity I have to speak with you alone."

The absurd shyness only increased at the husky undercurrent in his voice.

"We are hardly alone," she breathed, glancing toward the hundreds of guests moving through the open rooms.

"At least I have no dragon minding my every word."

A renegade smile twitched at her lips. Miss Stowe had proven to be a staunch companion, with a way of placing herself in locations such that Cassie's visitors never forgot she was present.

"Miss Stowe is a perfectly charming companion."

The blue gaze lingered on her traitorous mouth. "Perhaps, but I wish she were less diligent in her duties when I call," he complained as he stepped close enough for her to feel the heat of his body. "I am terrified that a misspoken word might have me tossed from the establishment."

She struggled to keep her thoughts from straying to the enticing scent of his cologne.

"You would only insist on being allowed back in."

He gave a low chuckle at her accusation.

"You are no doubt correct." His gaze shifted to her shoulder. "How do you feel?"

"I am well, thank you."

"The doctor called today?" he demanded.

Her expression became wry. She had no doubt who had insisted that the notable physician call on her. "As he has every day."

"There is no sign of infection?"

"None whatsoever."

"No stiffness in your shoulder?"

She felt a flutter of unease. She was unaccustomed to having anyone fussing over her in such a fashion. Not since her parents had been taken away. It was disconcerting, to say the least. With an awkward movement, she turned from his piercing regard.

"I have said I am fine," she insisted in low tones.

There was a faint pause as Lord Mumford studied her averted profile.

"Is there something troubling you?"

Suddenly frightened of the strange sensations that trembled through her body, she attempted to laugh in a light manner.

"A man attempted to kill me, a common

actress has stolen my estate, and an arrogant lord is incessantly interfering in my life. What is not troubling me?"

It was only with an effort that she resisted the need to watch his reaction to her ridiculous words.

"Do not fear, Miss Stanholte," he at last retorted in a carefully bland voice. "Soon enough you will be safely back in Devonshire. Far away from London and interfering lords."

The promise should have made her heart soar. It was all she had ever wanted. So why, then, did she feel the most absurd desire to cry?

It was a decided relief when her clouded gaze caught sight of the elderly woman imperiously beckoning from across the room.

"I believe that very determined lady is attempting to attract your attention."

Following her gaze, Lord Mumford muttered a low curse.

"Damn. I fear there is little use in ignoring Lady Radford. She will only continue that vulgar waving until I join her." His gaze shifted back in a warning manner. "I shall return in just a moment."

Cassie gave a vague nod, but even as Lord Mumford began to make his way toward the demanding Lady Radford, she was backing farther into the shadows and through the open French doors.

The room was hot and crowded, but, more importantly, Cassie felt an overpowering need to be on her own.

She had to control these ridiculous flights of fancy and recall precisely why she was in London.

It certainly was not to waste her evenings fluttering at the side of Lord Mumford.

Thirteen

The garden was a welcome relief after the smothering heat and noisy chatter of the ballroom. Sucking in the rose-scented air, Cassie moved through the maze of pathways, occasionally trailing a hand through a sparkling marble fountain or pausing to enjoy the scent of the spring blooms. She paid little heed to the direction she was taking. She only wished to regain the composure that had seemed so elusive since Lord Mumford had invaded her life.

Not that she held out much hope of success, she acknowledged with a sigh. Her composure seemed as elusive as her inheritance at the moment.

With every passing day, Lord Mumford inched his way further into her life. Every morning, she awoke and dressed with the knowledge he would be calling; every night she lay in her bed and recalled the moments he had held her in his arms. And more than once she had discovered herself forgetting the reason she had come to London when she was gazing into the depths of his blue eyes.

Lost in thought she wandered toward the

tall hedge that marked the end of the garden, where she caught sight of a small body hidden in the bushes. Her gaze narrowed as she felt an instinctive flare of fear. Clearly, someone was spying on the garden. As she forced herself to move forward, her suspicions were suddenly eased when she noted the grimy face of a young lad.

Smothering the urge to smile at the charmingly ugly countenance, Cassie instead conjured a forbidding frown.

"You there," she commanded in stern tones. "Come out at once."

"I ain't done nuthin'."

"I said at once."

There was the sound of snuffling; then with obvious reluctance the lad pushed his way out of the hedge and regarded her warily.

"You ain't goin' to hurt me?"

"Certainly not." Cassie felt a pang at the bony frame and unkempt hair. Poor child. He did not appear to have had a decent meal in days. "What are you doing here?"

His expression became even more wary. "I have a note for a bloke inside."

"A note? Then why did you not give it to the footman?"

"I am to give it meself. It be from his lady, Nell, upon a private matter."

A sudden suspicion gripped Cassie as she gazed down at the urchin.

"Who is the note for?"

His bottom lip jutted outward. "I ain't supposed to say."

Cassie battled to make her voice as calm as possible. "I can hardly help you if you will not tell me whom you wish to speak with."

He pondered her logic for a long moment, carefully studying her encouraging expression.

"Right enuf," he at last conceded. "I was suppose to find a bloke named Bidwell."

Cassie sucked in a sharp breath. A note for Lord Bidwell from Nell. It had to be Nell Maggert.

"Lord Bidwell?" she inquired with seeming innocence.

"That be the gent."

Cassie bent down in a conspiratorial manner. "You know, it would be much more sensible if you simply give me the note to take in to Lord Bidwell." She glanced through the hedge to the line of coaches waiting to be called. Clearly, the lad was keeping a guard on Lord Bidwell's coach so he could know when to dart from his hiding place and pass along the folded paper. She also noted the uniformed servants keeping close eyes on the streets as well as the house.

"After all, you do not wish to risk being run off by the servants."

The boy's eyes narrowed with innate cunning. "I don't know."

"Surely you do not wish to remain out here until Lord Bidwell departs? It could be hours."

He glanced toward the town house, his resolve wavering. "I can keep the quid?"

"Yes, indeed."

There was a brief pause; then with a startling quick motion he shoved the note into her hand and began burrowing his way back through the hedge.

"Can't say I ain't done me duty," he called.

Glancing down at the now crumpled note, Cassie wrestled with her conscience. Common manners assured her that it was indecent to pry into private correspondence. But over the past weeks she had been forced to put aside more delicate sensibilities. Indeed, reading another's correspondence was becoming more a habit than a sin. Pressing aside the image of her mother's disapproving face, Cassie unfolded the note and tilted it toward a nearby lamp.

In the flickering light, it was difficult to translate the uneven writing. At last she managed to make sense of the scratchings.

I must meet with you tonight, but not at the house. I fear it is being watched.
Come to the theater.

Nell

Theater. Any lingering sense of guilt was doused as Cassie felt a flare of pure fury. They had found Nell Maggert. They had found her and not said a word to her.

The sheer arrogance made her long to sweep back into the ballroom and demand that Lord Mumford and his friend confess the truth. But the knowledge that they would only shrug aside her anger and blithely reassure her that they would take care of everything kept her in the shadowed garden.

Nell would be at a theater, tonight and Cassie was quite certain it was the same theater where the actress had once worked.

This was the perfect opportunity for Cassie to confront the woman and force her to confess the truth about Liza.

Without giving herself time to ponder the danger of her impulsive decision, Cassie moved back through the twisted paths, avoiding the large terrace and choosing instead a smaller path that led toward the side of the house. Within moments, she managed to catch sight of a uniformed footman who was no doubt eluding the stern eye of the housekeeper. Hearing her approach, the young man hastily straightened and attempted to appear as if he were supposed to be hiding in the shadows.

"Good evening, miss."

"I need your assistance."

"Yes?"

Drawing in a steadying breath, Cassie gathered her fraying courage.

"Please locate Miss Stowe and inform her that Miss Stanholte has acquired a headache and has gone home. She can ride with Lady Pembroke."

"Very good."

"And have my coachman meet me in the front."

With a bow, the footman scurried to follow her commands. Cassie, on the other hand, waited several moments before ducking through a side door and cautiously making her way to the front entrance.

She was well aware that she needed to avoid Lord Mumford and the devious Lord Bidwell. They were bound to be suspicious of her sudden illness. And she had no desire to face their unnerving questions.

Thankfully, her carriage was swift to arrive, and hurrying down the staircase, she allowed the servant to help her into the cushioned seat. She gave the startled groom concise orders to drive to the theater before breathing a sigh of relief.

This time no one would stop her from speaking with Nell Maggert, she told herself sternly. She would at last have the truth she had been searching for.

Unconsciously twisting her fingers in her lap as they left the elegant neighborhoods behind and traveled to the narrow, cramped street in front of the theater, Cassie suddenly shuddered as they pulled to a halt. Regardless of Lord Mumford's accusations that she possessed no sense, she had not forgotten her numerous frights over the past few weeks. She intended to be very careful on this occasion.

Allowing herself to be handed down, she quietly commanded the groom to remain with the carriage. She did not notice the older servant glancing up the street or his abrupt wave to a thin gentleman climbing out of his own carriage. She was far too occupied with controlling her racing heart as she approached the open doors to the theater.

Rancorous noise and off-key music spilled onto the street as Cassie approached, and she briefly hesitated. Would Nell be inside the theater? Or was she hidden nearby and waiting for the arrival of Lord Bidwell?

Cassie wavered; then, squaring her shoulders, she prepared herself to enter the theater. It could be no more dangerous than remaining in the dark streets. But even as she prepared to move forward, there was a sudden footstep behind her. Cassie froze; then a scream rose to her throat as a rough hand closed over her throat and an arm wrapped about her waist, pinning her arms to her sides.

Oh, Lord, not again, she thought with a surge of panic.

Would she never learn?

The young footman watched Lord Mumford pace across the salon with a wary gaze. Although he was commanded by the housekeeper to ensure the late night visitor's comfort, he was wisely reluctant to call attention to his presence. The gentleman had been obviously shaken when he had arrived a quarter of an hour before to discover Miss Stanholte had not yet returned home. And the sharpening tension in his elegant features warned that his unease was edged with a mounting fury.

Still, the young man was well aware it was no more wise to stir the ire of the decidedly large housekeeper. His ears had been boxed on more than one occasion. So with an inward sigh, he reluctantly stepped forward.

"Can I offer you something to drink, my lord?"

With an effort, Luke forced himself to halt his restless pacing and turn toward the waiting servant.

"What?"

"I asked if you would like something to drink. Sherry or perhaps tea?"

"Brandy," he demanded in clipped tones.

"Of course."

"And I wish to speak with Miss Stanholte the moment she arrives."

"Very good."

With obvious haste, the servant gave a bow and backed from the room. Luke made a rueful grimace. He did not intend to punish hapless servants with his temper, but he was discovering it increasingly difficult to maintain command of his emotions.

The devil take Cassandra Stanholte.

When the servant had arrived with the message that Miss Stanholte had called for her carriage, he had been only faintly alarmed. Over the last few days, he had noted her antagonism toward him being slowly replaced by a bewildered awareness.

He had also sensed that she was attempting to deny her unfamiliar reactions. He had presumed her flight tonight had been one of panic. Now he realized that she was up to something far more devious.

Or worse, that the scar-faced gentleman had once again struck.

His heart twisted with sharp fear, and he battled the urge to rush out of the house and search for the impossible woman. It would be foolish to stumble about London with no notion of where she might be.

Unconsciously clenching his hands, Luke resisted the urge to call for the servant. Had the fool been forced to travel to France for the brandy? Then he gave a shake of his head. The poor man was probably hiding in the cellar in the hopes that Luke would disappear before he would be forced to return. Suddenly the sound of a door closing, followed by the muffled sound of voices, had him stiffening in a combination of dread and anticipation.

He was barely aware that he was holding his breath as he turned to face the door. He breathed again in a rush of disappointment at the sight of the narrow countenance of Lord Bidwell.

"Good God. Biddles."

With a sardonic smile, Biddles offered

him an elaborate bow. "Good evening, Mumford."

"What the devil are you doing here?"

"Returning something I believe you have misplaced."

Stepping to one side of the door, the small gentleman waved to someone still in the hallway. Luke gave a startled exclamation as a hulking servant entered carrying a furious Miss Stanholte.

"Unhand me, you . . . beast," she demanded, her small countenance red with fury.

A fierce surge of relief raced through Luke even as he regarded the uncontrollable minx with mounting anger.

This infuriating woman was going to land him in Bedlam.

"Where did you find her?" Luke demanded.

"Her groom possessed the good sense to leave word that Miss Stanholte had demanded her carriage, and my own groom came to warn me," Biddles said. "We decided to follow." He turned to meet the glittering gaze of Miss Stanholte. "Imagine my surprise when we traveled directly to Toby's nasty little theater."

Her chin only tilted. "You had no right to interfere."

With a shrug, Biddles returned his attention to Luke. "She unfortunately refused to be rescued without a struggle."

Caught between the desire to throttle the young lady and kiss her senseless, Luke stabbed her with a narrowed gaze.

"You went to that neighborhood in the middle of the night? Alone?" He gave a disbelieving shake of his head. "Why do you not simply slit your own throat and save Toby the trouble?"

Predictably, she refused to show an ounce of remorse for her illogical behavior.

"I went to that theater because I caught a young boy in the garden tonight waiting with a note for Lord Bidwell," she retorted in furious tones. "A note from Nell Maggert."

"Egad, Miss Stanholte." With a languid motion, Biddles lifted his quizzing glass. "Do you always go about reading private notes?"

"I suspected you were hiding information from me." Her accusing gaze shifted from Biddles to Luke. "How long have you known where she lives?"

Luke was forced to smother a ridiculous prick of guilt. Why should he feel as if he were in the wrong when he was merely attempting to save her from her own stupidity? Tonight's absurd performance had only proven he had been correct to keep the information to himself. This foolish chit could not be trusted not to get herself killed.

"Only a few days."

"Why did you not tell me?"

"Because I suspected that you would behave in precisely this absurd fashion."

Wrapping her arms about her waist, she regarded him with a condemning expression.

"I should have been told."

His anger returned as he regarded the tiny frame and pale face surrounded by the golden curls that had tumbled free. Why couldn't she understand? The mere thought of allowing her to place herself in danger was enough to keep him lying awake at night. He had to protect her, even if it was from herself.

"This is no game, Miss Stanholte, even if you are determined to treat it as if it is."

"I am well aware this is no game, Lord Mumford. I am the one who has been forced from her home and in danger of losing everything I hold dear."

"And you think risking your neck at every opportunity is going to change that?"

Her eyes widened with fury, but even as

her mouth opened to slay him with her decidedly wicked tongue, Biddles was interrupting. A wise man, he realized that it was time to make a strategic retreat.

"Yes, this is all quite charming, but I believe I shall toddle off to my club. I limit myself to rescuing one damsel per evening, don't you know." He performed a deep bow. "Your servant."

They watched in silence as the slender gentleman swept from the room closely guarded by the large servant. Then, with a jerky motion, Miss Stanholte turned to regard Luke with a frown.

"Why are you even here? I should think you would be at the ball."

"When I discovered you had left, I feared that you had become ill," he smoothly retorted, not bothering to mention his hope that it was her softening emotions toward him that had been responsible for her abrupt flight.

If she did possess a change of heart in regard to him, it was not evident in her rigid expression.

"So you risk a scandal by arriving at such an hour?"

"Hardly as scandalous as a young lady trotting about London at this hour," he retorted, his frayed nerves not improved by the thought of what might have occurred if Biddles had not followed the carriage.

"I would not need to . . . trot about London at this hour if you had simply told me the truth."

"Biddles is perfectly capable of discovering whatever information Nell might possess. Indeed, he has made remarkable progress with the actress. The last thing he needs is you rushing in and startling the nervous woman into flight. Did you ever think of that?"

Clearly unable to argue the logic of his argument, Cassandra abruptly turned away from his piercing scrutiny.

"I am in no mood to argue with you further. It is late and I am tired. So, if you will excuse me —"

"No." Luke strode forward to grasp her elbow and turn her back to face him. Did she expect him to meekly stand aside while she courted danger with such blatant disregard? "We are not finished with this, Cassie."

Not seeming to notice his familiar manner of speech, she met his burning gaze with stubborn courage. "It is, as far as I am concerned."

"I will not allow you to place yourself at risk again. If you are too foolish to protect yourself, then I will."

"Really? And how do you propose to do that?"

"I will lock you in a dungeon if necessary."

"Indeed." The gray eyes darkened with a dangerous light. "I should like to see you try."

His gaze abruptly dropped to the stubborn line of her mouth. Lord, how he longed to press her against his body, to wrap her in his arms and never let her go.

"Or perhaps I will simply marry you," he threatened in husky tones.

Cassandra's soft gasp was muffled as a loud cry sounded in the doorway. With a sense of shock, Luke slowly raised his head to discover his Aunt Sophia and Miss Stowe standing just inside the room. And judging from the delighted expression on Sophia's countenance, she had clearly heard the words intended only for Cassandra.

"Marriage. Did you hear that, Anne? Our two lovebirds have at last decided to wed. What glorious news. I must return to the carriage at once to tell Lord Pembroke."

Uncertain why he felt nothing but satisfaction, Luke made no effort to halt the retreating form of his aunt. Indeed, he was quite certain a battalion of French soldiers could not have halted her at the moment. Instead, he glanced down at Cassandra's horrified countenance with a slow smile.

Fourteen

Feeling much like one of the poor beasts caged at the Tower of London, Cassie paced through the salon with a simmering panic.

What the devil was she going to do?

Last night she had dared to hope that she would at last discover Nell Maggert and put this whole horrible situation behind her. Instead, she had been arrogantly kidnapped by Lord Bidwell and then chastised as if she were a particularly dim-witted child by Lord Mumford.

And to make matters worse, Lady Pembroke now believed she was actually engaged to marry the arrogant earl.

It was . . . absurd.

She turned about to head in the other direction when the uniformed butler silently glided into the room.

"Lady Pembroke to see you, Miss Stanholte."

Cassie felt the color drain from her face at the quiet announcement. She couldn't face Lady Pembroke. Not until Luke had managed to straighten out the horrible muddle he had created. But even as she sorted through her foggy mind for a reasonable excuse to fob the woman off, Lady Pembroke swept into the room with a beaming smile.

"My dearest Cassandra," she purred, determinedly planting a kiss on her cheek before pulling back to admire her pale yellow muslin gown.

Cassie flushed with discomfort. "Lady Pembroke."

"I realize that you must have any number of things to attend to today, but I had to speak with you."

"Oh?"

"First, you must know how sincerely delighted I am that you are to wed Luke."

Cassie longed to sink beneath the floorboards. She had never felt more embarrassed in her life. She steeled her nerves to confess the truth.

"But, my lady —"

"Tut, tut, Aunt Sophia now," she interrupted with a smile.

Cassie swallowed a sigh of exasperation. "Very well, Aunt Sophia. The truth of the matter is —"

"Please, let me finish, my dear," Aunt Sophia once again interrupted, clearly unaware of Cassie's growing discomfort. "For the past few years I have become increasingly concerned about Luke. He seemed unable to settle himself. Even after receiving his inheritance, he was restless and dissatisfied with life. It was as if he were searching for something he could not find. But now he has found what he was searching for. You."

A peculiar pang twisted Cassie's heart. Almost as if she regretted that Sophia's words were not true. That she wanted to be what Luke needed in his life.

"Oh."

"You know, you remind me very much of Luke's mother. The same kindness and natural graciousness, and certainly the same spirited nature." Ignoring the painful heat staining Cassie's cheeks, Sophia opened her reticule to withdraw a small box, which she slowly opened. "Which is why she would have wanted me to give you this."

With a sinking heart, Cassie regarded the delicate pearl necklace lying on a bed of satin. It was exquisite, with each pearl perfectly matching the next and the clasp made of silver and small diamonds. Cassie gave a hasty shake of her head.

"Oh, please, I cannot accept such a gift."

"Do not be a goose. It is what Bella would have wanted," Sophia gently chastised. "Now, I shall leave it to Luke to discuss the marriage settlement, but be assured that I have already made the announcement for the newspaper. And since you have no close family member to assist you, I hope very much you will do me the honor and allow me to act in your mother's stead."

A ridiculous surge of tears filled Cassie's eyes at the kind offer. She wished the noblewoman had stormed in with a furious refusal to approve of the marriage of her precious nephew to a country nobody. At least then it would have been a simple matter to deny that she had any intentions of wedding the aggravating lord. Now she felt like a thorough villain as she prepared to disappoint the older lady.

"I . . . Aunt Sophia —"

"Just think upon it, my dear," Sophia said, clearly misreading her embarrassment. "Now I must go. I have an endless number of calls to make this morning. Such wonderful news."

Reaching out her hand, Sophia thrust the box into Cassie's nerveless fingers. Then, with a last smile, she turned to march from the room as abruptly as she had entered.

Left on her own, Cassie muttered an inelegant curse. How could she have been such a coward? She should have insisted that Sophia listen to her. Now the lady was off to announce a wedding that was never going to occur.

Against her will, Cassie's gaze dropped to the delicate pearls glowing in the lined box. The necklace was lovely. Unlike many older necklaces, it was simply designed, with no added sets to distract from the elegant style. A necklace her own mother would have chosen.

It also belonged to the lady whom Lord Mumford would eventually claim as his bride.

That odd pang once again twisted her heart as she studied the delicate pearls. Somehow the thought was uncannily disturbing, as if the knowledge that Lord Mumford would one day choose a beautiful young bride were a source of pain.

Angered by her queer reaction, Cassie frowned down at the box, attempting to decide what she should do with the unwelcome gift. She was still undecided when she was once more interrupted by the entrance of her stoic-faced butler.

Good Lord, what now?

"Lord Mumford."

So . . . at last he had decided to make an appearance, she seethed. Too late to confront his aunt. Well, this entire disaster was his fault. He could bloody well make it right.

"Please show him in."

"Very good."

The butler bowed his way out and within the blink of an eye returned with her visitor. Just for a moment Cassie allowed her gaze to linger on the handsome countenance and the well-defined form so faithfully revealed by the fitted coat and breeches. Even though she had met a hundred gentlemen since arriving in London, not one could compare with this man. Somehow they all seemed a pale shadow when he was near.

No doubt because he was always managing to infuriate her, she sternly reminded herself.

Titling her chin to a militant angle, she eyed him with a frown.

"Where have you been?"

With a lazy smile, Luke strolled into the room.

"Is that any way to greet your soon-to-be husband?"

"This is no jesting manner, sir," she retorted in sour tones.

"No?"

The annoying . . . toad, she simmered. How could he stand there with smug amusement as if there were nothing at all the matter?

Hoping to shake that indomitable composure, she thrust out her hand to reveal the small box.

"Your aunt just brought me this."

He lifted his quizzing glass to regard the pearl necklace. "Ah, my mother's necklace."

"Precisely."

"It is only a small token." He gave a faint shrug. "There are any number of jewels among my mother's things, as well as the Mumford diamonds that will be yours upon our marriage. Unless, of course, you wish to have something else commissioned? Emeralds, perhaps?"

She stamped a tiny foot as her frustration became too much.

"Stop this foolishness at once."

He possessed the arrogance to give a low chuckle. "What do you wish me to do?"

Several delightfully rude comments floated through her mind.

"Speak with your aunt and tell her this is all a terrible mistake," she demanded.

"Unfortunately, things have gone too far for that."

"What?"

"My aunt has already managed to spread the announcement of our impending wedding throughout the greater part of London." He lifted his slender hands in a helpless motion. "By this evening it should be well on its way through Europe. If we claim there is no wedding, then we shall all appear to be fools."

She gave a disbelieving shake of her head.

"What are you suggesting?"

"That we allow this engagement to continue," he smoothly responded.

Cassie widened her eyes in shock, quite certain that he could not be completely sane. Surely he was not actually suggesting that they go through with this ridiculous engagement?

"Have you taken a blow to the head?"

His lips twitched at her sharp accusation. "Not recently."

"Then you must realize that it is absurd."

An undeniable emotion flickered through the dark blue eyes before he was lifting a negligent shoulder.

"Actually, after some consideration, I realized that it is a perfect means of allowing me to be at your side." His smile twisted as a flare of panic rippled over her expressive countenance. "At least until we have captured the villain attempting to steal your inheritance."

Quite certain that she must still be abed and in the midst of a terrible nightmare, Cassie pressed a hand to her uneven heart.

"And then?"

"Then you return to Devonshire, and in

due time I announce that you have had second thoughts."

Cassie shivered. As he had with all his ludicrous suggestions, he made it all sound so reasonable. Just a harmless ploy for the next few days. But she was swiftly learning that nothing was as simple as it appeared with this man.

With every seemingly innocent gesture, he had managed to wiggle his way more firmly into her life. Into her every thought. Even now she feared that she would never be truly free of his memory.

She shivered again as she took a hasty step back.

"No, I cannot."

He lifted his brows at her fierce tone, but an oddly satisfied smile curved his mouth.

"Why?"

She swiftly searched for a logical excuse. "I cannot lie to your aunt."

"You have been lying since you arrived in London," he pointed out in reasonable tones.

"This is different," she muttered.

He stepped forward, his hand unexpectedly reaching out to cup her chin in a gentle grasp.

"It is only for a few days."

A dizzying heat spread through her body.

"Oh," she breathed, her gaze locking

with his darkened eyes.

Just for a moment, they regarded one another in silence. A breathless excitement clutched at Cassie. Almost against her will, her body swayed forward, her lips parting. With a husky murmur, Luke slowly lowered his head to capture her mouth in a soft, lingering kiss. Cassie's knees quivered as sweet sensations trembled through her body. She wanted to press herself even closer. To have his arms wrap about her and never let her go.

Never let her go . . .

A flare of panic sliced through her mounting passion, and with a tiny moan, she abruptly pulled away from his enticing kiss.

What was happening to her?

She felt . . . bewitched. Unable to think of anything beyond her growing need to be with this man.

As if sensing the chaotic emotions battling within her heart, with a rueful smile Luke reached out to stroke her cheek.

"Do not fear, Cassandra," he said in low tones. "Everything will be well."

She could say nothing as he gave a bow, then turned to move out of the room.

Her lips still trembled from the heat of his kiss and her knees still threatened to buckle.

269

And she was quite, quite certain that nothing would ever be well again.

Leaving Miss Stanholte's town house, Luke ordered his groom to head for Lord Bidwell's. He had received a message earlier from his friend, but nothing could distract him from calling upon Cassandra the moment he arose. Now he could only wonder at his own sanity.

Had he truly insisted that the small hellion become his fiancée?

It seemed impossible.

After all, he was a gentleman who devoted his time to avoiding the parson's trap, not dragging unwilling, sharp-tongued chits to the nearest vicar. Still, when he had said the impetuous words last evening and his aunt had assumed he had been proposing, he had realized that he wanted nothing more than to claim Cassandra as his wife.

Perhaps he was losing what few senses he still possessed.

Leaning back in his seat, Luke closed his eyes. The sweet scent of violets clung to his clothing, sending a shiver of fierce need through his body. How he longed to drown himself in her innocence, to sweep her into his arms and tutor her in the delights of passion.

He wanted her to belong to him forever.

Unfortunately, the lady had made it painfully clear that she considered an engagement to him as enjoyable as being stricken by the plague. An odd predicament, considering he was once toasted as the most eligible gentleman in all of England.

The carriage rolled to a halt, and, still dwelling on his dark thoughts, Luke stepped out and hurried up the stairs and through the door held open by the waiting butler. Within moments, he was being led to an Egyptian-styled salon.

Leaning against the mantel, Biddles regarded his friend's deep frown with an arched brow.

"Ah . . . the happy bridegroom," he drawled. "Welcome."

Luke grimaced, only vaguely surprised that the gentleman had managed to discover the rumors of his engagement so swiftly.

"Hardly happy," he retorted.

The brow arched even higher. "Egad, you are not having troubles already?"

"There has been nothing but troubles since Miss Stanholte so disobligingly tossed herself beneath my carriage."

With a smooth movement, Biddles crossed to pour two glasses of brandy; then moving to Luke, he thrust one into his hand.

"You appear in need of reinforcement."

Luke willingly accepted the brandy, for once not bothering to disguise his inner emotions.

"Why must she be so . . . impossible?"

"Indeed," Biddles murmured.

"There are any number of ladies who would be delighted at being engaged to the Earl of Mumford."

"Certainly."

Luke took a healthy gulp of the fiery spirit.

"And it is not as if she were completely indifferent to me," he complained, recalling her trembling reaction to his kiss.

"No."

"So why will she not accept that I am simply doing what is best for her?"

Biddles gave an elegant shrug, his expression suspiciously bland.

"Ungrateful wench."

"Precisely."

"One would think she would appreciate having you thrust your way into her life, threaten her with exposure if she does not move into a home of your choosing, and then blackmail her into becoming your fiancée."

Luke gave a startled blink at the sudden attack. Really, he had always considered

Biddles his friend. He needn't make it all sound so . . . arrogant.

"Would she have preferred that I stand aside and allow her to be killed?"

Unrepentant, Biddles lifted his shrewd gaze to stab Luke with a piercing regard.

"Perhaps she would prefer not to be protected with such . . . enthusiasm."

"And what is that supposed to mean?"

"Merely that Miss Stanholte is a woman of considerable spirit," Biddles retorted in smooth tones. "She is bound to shy away from a rein held too tightly."

Luke angrily opened his mouth to protest, only to have the angry words falter at the realization his friend was right.

He had always known that Cassandra was not a lady who could be bullied or forced into anything. She had been her own mistress for far too long. It was perhaps one of the things that he most admired about her. And yet, he had attempted to control and manipulate her since she had crashed into his life.

"Why does it all have to be so bloody complicated?" he growled in frustration.

"Love is always complicated." Biddles lifted his glass in a mocking toast. "Which is why I prefer lust."

"Love."

The word was jerked from Luke with a faint sense of shock. He should be horrified by the accusation. Love was for fools. That was what he had always told himself. And even though he had known perhaps from the moment he had laid eyes upon Cassandra that he desired her, it was just within the past few days that he had accepted it as far more than mere desire.

Love.

Quite extraordinary.

"You have my fullest sympathy," Biddles offered with an impish grin.

"Oddly enough, I have never been happier." He gave a wry grimace. "Of course, I have never been so miserable either."

Biddles set aside his glass. "What will you do?"

"What can I do?" Luke set aside his own glass and wearily ran a hand over the back of his neck. It had been far too long since he had enjoyed a peaceful night's rest, let alone a day without one worry or another. And always in the back of his mind was the terrifying knowledge he would eventually lose Cassandra, either to the devious plot of the scar-faced gentleman or to the remote isolation of her Devonshire estate. "Even if I manage to force Miss Stanholte into marriage, she would only resent me."

Biddles tilted his head to one side. "Have you considered telling her how you feel?"

Luke gave a dry laugh. "And frighten her even more?"

"As you said, she is not indifferent to you."

"No." A brief, searing image of Cassandra in his arms sent a flare of desire through his body. Good Lord, he was reacting like a mere greenhorn. A most discomforting sensation. With an effort, he firmly turned his thoughts to his reason for coming to the town house in the first place. "But first we must ensure she is safe. What have you discovered?"

With a decidedly smug smile, Biddles returned to his post beside the mantel.

"I happened to catch up with the delightful Nell last evening, and she confessed that she is deeply concerned about a friend who is in a decided quandary."

"Indeed?" Luke narrowed his gaze. "And did you offer your assistance?"

Biddles pretended an interest in the cuff of his coat. "I assured her I could only be of help if I knew the full details."

"But of course." Luke refused to allow his hopes to be raised. He had been disappointed on too many occasions. "And what did she say?"

"She said that this friend had married a gentleman who claimed to be the illegitimate son of Lord Stanholte."

"Lord Stanholte." Luke sucked in a sharp breath. "Miss Stanholte's father?"

"Grandfather," Biddles corrected. "It seems that the older Lord Stanholte kept his mistress in a nearby cottage, and when she produced a son, he ensured that the boy received a small allowance from the estate and a proper education. He also sent both of them to London when he tired of the young lady. Unfortunately, when the old man died, the illegitimate son presented himself in Devonshire and demanded a share of the inheritance." Biddles lifted his gaze. "Needless to say, the new lord promptly declined the gentleman's request, and after a rather nasty fight, during which the chap received a cut to the face, he was sent on his way. He left swearing he would have his revenge."

Luke abruptly released his breath. Although he had been quite certain the mysterious gentleman had a connection to the Stanholte family, he had not suspected that it would be so close. He now realized why the man was so ruthlessly determined. This gentleman had clearly convinced himself that Stanholte Estate should be his.

"So, we now comprehend why he chose

Miss Stanholte and how he knew about the missing uncle," he murmured.

"What we do not know is how to find him," Biddles pointed out.

Luke nodded. They were close, but not close enough.

"A few days ago I convinced Toby to lead me through the neighborhood where he claimed he had followed his employer," Luke revealed. "Perhaps we should return for a closer inspection."

"Ah, Toby." Biddles smiled in a dangerous manner. "How is the little rat?"

Luke chuckled as he recalled his unwilling guest's bitter reproaches.

"Sadly disappointed with his accommodations."

"He should consider himself fortunate you found him before I did," Biddles said. Before he could continue, there was the sound of raised voices and a loud crash. "What the devil?"

With a sense of shock, Luke turned just as the door was thrust open to reveal the leathered countenance of Cassandra's groom.

Luke's heart came to a complete halt as the man stepped forward.

"My lord," the servant breathed, his uniform torn and in disarray. "You must come at once."

Fifteen

Rushing into the room with a distinct lack of his usual composure, the butler performed a hasty bow.

"I am sorry, Lord Bidwell," the servant apologized, turning to glare at the rattled groom. "This man slipped through the servants' door before he could be halted."

Biddles waved a dismissive hand. "Do not fear; we will see him."

With another bow, the butler backed out of the room, clearly accustomed to his employer's peculiar habits.

Luke paid no heed to anything but the lined face of Cassandra's groom.

"What has occurred?" he demanded in rough tones.

"It is Miss Stanholte," he breathed.

Luke's heart clenched in agony. "Where is she? Has she been harmed?"

"I cannot say." The groom twisted his battered hat in a nervous fashion, his eyes dark with concern. "We were on our way to Hatcher's when a carriage pulled beside us. Before I could guess what was occurring, two villains pulled Miss Stanholte and Miss Stowe from our carriage and shoved them into the one beside us. I tried to follow, but they ran us from the road." His voice broke with suppressed emotion. "Forgive me, my lord."

Luke did not doubt for a moment this man had done everything in his power to save Miss Stanholte. Still, his fear was too powerful to protect this man's pride.

"There is no time for that." He abruptly turned to the silent Lord Bidwell. "Come, Biddles."

The thin gentleman remained unflappable.

"Where are we headed?" he demanded with annoying logic. "We do not know where Miss Stanholte was being taken."

Luke dampened his instinctive flare of anger, knowing his friend was simply attempting to keep a level head.

"We will begin with the theater and then move to the neighborhood beyond."

Biddles ran a finger down the side of his long nose. "That could take hours."

"I do not care if it will take days," Luke snapped. "I will find her."

Biddles smiled with dry humor. "I merely meant we will need help. You go ahead, and I will meet you as soon as I am able."

"Very well." Luke gave a decisive nod of his head, then returned his attention to the groom. "I want you to go to the theater. I will begin in the neighborhood."

"Yes, my lord."

Without waiting for any further discussion, Luke strode out of the house and down the front walk. Then motioning to Jameson, he gave his orders in crisp tones.

Climbing into the carriage, he was forced to contain his rising panic as the groom battled his way through the heavy traffic. A dozen images of Cassandra in dire need flickered through his vivid imagination, each worse than the other.

He at last reined in his wayward thoughts. He would rescue her before it was too late. He had to rescue her.

Gritting his teeth, Luke impatiently waited for the carriage to come to a halt in a seedy neighborhood. Jumping out, he directed Jameson toward a row of unkempt shops while he turned toward what appeared to be an abandoned school.

Toby had claimed to have tracked the scar-faced man to this narrow street before losing sight of him. Luke had no better clue as to where to begin his search, so he marched to the ramshackle building and began making his way through the shadows.

In the distance he could hear the squall of

a hungry baby and the shouts of children at play, but close at hand there was a peculiar silence. No voices, no movement, not even the bark of a dog. That fact alone made him wonder if there was something, or someone, near keeping the place clear of strays.

Frustratingly, however, he had nearly circled the entire building without evidence that anyone had been near the place in years, when something shimmered in the pale dust.

With a frown, Luke bent down to pick up the tiny round object. His heart gave a sudden leap as he realized that he was holding a perfect pearl.

Cassandra . . .

Cautiously pressing himself against the building, Luke began inching toward a door half hanging from its hinges. He bent twice more to pick up pearls, inwardly congratulating Cassandra on her quick thinking. Clearly, she had realized that she must leave some clue as to her whereabouts and had used the only things available. His mother's pearls had never been more beautiful.

Halting beside the door, Luke was suddenly aware of the sound of muted voices.

"I don't like the thought of killing the lass," a rough male voice complained, making Luke stiffen.

"No one says yer to think," another voice argued.

"What if we be caught? It'll be the hangman's noose."

"Just keep yer eyes open."

"I ain't paid enough fer the noose," the first man grumbled.

"Yer more likely to get a bullet if yer don't mind yerself."

"I still don't like it."

"Yer will like it even less if the guv hears yer. Now shut yer yap and watch the door."

Cassandra was inside. And for the moment she was still alive. It was all he needed.

Silently turning, he went in search of Jameson.

Ignoring the splinters ripping at her tender skin, Cassie desperately pulled at the boards covering the window.

"Please, Miss Cassie, you will hurt yourself," Miss Stowe pleaded from a dark corner.

With a reluctant sigh, Cassie leaned her head against the cold stone. It had been less than an hour since the men had appeared from nowhere and forced her and Miss Stowe into the carriage, but she felt as if it was a lifetime.

For weeks she had barely avoided the

traps of her mysterious pursuer. And all along she had known he would eventually succeed if she did not discover him first. Now the worst had happened, and she was far from certain that she possessed the strength to survive.

"We must do something," she muttered.

The older woman shivered as she sat on the rickety chair. It was the only piece of furniture in the cramped room besides a broken desk.

"Who are these men?"

Cassie felt a stab of guilt as she turned to glance at her companion. Poor woman. All Miss Stowe had wanted was a brief respite from her tyrannical brother and the opportunity to attend a few elegant parties. She had no notion she was placing herself in such danger.

"I do not know," Cassie murmured, only half lying.

"Tut, tut. I am injured, Miss Stanholte," a male voice drawled. With a gasp, Cassie turned to discover a tall, dark-haired man standing in the doorway. "As one of your few surviving relatives, I thought you might remember me."

Relative? Cassie stepped backward in distaste.

"Who are you?"

His thin lips twisted in a mocking smile. "You do not recall my visit to your home?"

Once again Cassie had a brief, troubling image of a dark-haired man standing with her father. She had been peering through the window and had overheard the angry words and then . . . yes, she remembered. Her father had demanded the man leave, and he had suddenly pulled a knife. There had been a struggle, and the intruder had been cut on the cheek. She also remembered the servants forcibly hauling the man from the estate.

"You were no guest in my home," she retorted.

His eyes narrowed in an ugly manner. "No, you are right. I was no guest, but I am as much a Stanholte as you, my dear niece." He watched in pleasure as her eyes widened in shock. "Unfortunately, I have never been allowed the same luxuries as yourself. I was forced to endure on a pittance, while you were lavished with every comfort you might desire." His smooth tone roughened with deep bitterness. "I was raised in secrecy and shame, while you were allowed your privileged place in Society."

Cassie's fear only deepened. There was something extraordinarily evil in his cold eyes.

"What do you want?" she breathed.

"Everything."

"Everything?"

With deadly purpose, he strolled across the broken floor to tower above her stiff body.

"Everything that should have been mine. You see, I might once have been satisfied with a mere portion of the inheritance, but your father proved that Stanholtes are incapable of sharing. So I will take it all."

With an effort, Cassie prevented herself from cowering beneath his glittering gaze.

"You sent Liza to Devonshire," she accused.

"Of course." He did not even bother to deny his treachery. "I had heard my father often lament the loss of his eldest child. It seemed only fitting that I grant his dearest desire and discover the whereabouts of the prodigal son."

Although Cassie only vaguely recalled her grandfather, she found it difficult to conceive that he could have produced a child so lacking in conscience. This man was an insult to the Stanholte name.

"You discovered nothing," she gritted.

His smile merely widened at her overt distaste.

"Ah, but Liza has so successfully convinced your Man of Business that we have. And once you have conveniently disappeared, then there will be nothing to stand in our way."

"You are wrong." She tilted her chin to a defiant angle. "Lord Mumford and Lord Bidwell both know the truth."

A sudden, fierce flare of fury rippled over his handsome features.

"They can prove nothing."

"They will see you in Newgate."

His hands clenched as if he was barely resisting the urge to hit her.

"Be silent," he commanded.

"Or you will harm me?" she demanded. Despite the fear clutching at her stomach, Cassie battled to face him squarely. He would never have the satisfaction of seeing her beg. "You must realize that this is all too late. You will never gain control of Stanholte Estate. No matter what happens to me."

"It will be mine." The scar stood out in pale contrast to his flushed skin. "It belongs to me."

"Never."

His hand rose, and Cassie prepared herself for the coming blow, but before it could land, a large, pock marked man stumbled into the room.

"Guv."

With a low snarl, the villain turned to stab the intruder with a murderous glare.

"What is it?"

The man blanched in fear. "Men approaching."

"Are you certain they are coming here?"

"Aye."

"Get my carriage," he snapped. Cassie felt a surge of hope that was swiftly snatched away as her captor reached into the pocket of his coat to withdraw a pistol. "It seems this is good-bye, my dear."

A sense of irony struck Cassie as she watched the barrel of the gun point directly at her heart. It was becoming a familiar sight, and once again there was nothing she could do to prevent the horrible end. Then, without warning, Miss Stowe suddenly jumped to her feet.

"No! Stop!" she screamed.

Instinctively, the man turned toward the older woman, and Cassie knew in a heartbeat he would kill her without a second thought. She couldn't allow the woman to be harmed.

Not giving herself time to think, Cassie gritted her teeth and with all her might ran forward and bowled straight into the unsuspecting cad. A loud shot retorted through the room as Cassie hit the floor with a heavy thud.

Just for a moment, the world seemed to whirl about her head and she battled to maintain consciousness. She could not afford to black out now. But the blow to her head proved too great, and even as she struggled to remain awake, a heavy darkness rushed up to greet her.

After what might have been minutes or hours, Cassie at last pried open her heavy lids to make the shocking discovery she was being held tight in the arms of Lord Mumford and he was stroking her hair in the most intimate fashion.

"Cassie . . . Cassie, my love," he murmured as her gaze fluttered upward. "Are you harmed?"

She took a moment to realize she was settled on Luke's lap and that the room was strangely empty. She also realized that the warmth of his body was creating a very delightful tingle of pleasure through her weak form.

"No, I do not think so," she replied, attempting to focus her fuzzy thoughts. "What of Miss Stowe?"

His beloved countenance was pale and tight with the need to control his emotions.

"She is shaken, but unharmed."

"Thank God." Cassie breathed a sigh of relief. She had been terrified she had been too late. Then a small frown tugged at her brow. "How did you find me?"

"Your groom came to say that you had been kidnapped. I knew approximately where the scoundrel was hiding, but without your pearls I would never have gotten here in time."

Cassie felt a pang of remorse. When the men had dragged her toward the abandoned building, she realized that no one would think to search for her in such a place. Not without some clue that she was within. She had nothing to drop that would not also attract the attention of her captors, until she recalled the delicate pearls that hung about her neck. She had known that Luke would immediately recognize the pearls. Just as she had known he would come for her.

"Your mother's beautiful pearls," she sighed.

"It does not matter. I will buy you another necklace. A dozen necklaces."

An abrupt shudder wracked her slender frame. Even now, wrapped in his arms, she could not believe that she was safe.

"I was so frightened."

His arms tightened. "You have no need to ever be frightened again, my love."

"That man . . ." Her eyes darkened at the memory of her kidnapper. "He said he was my uncle."

He grimaced at her trembling words. "Yes, I know."

"He said he deserved my inheritance."

"He was clearly unbalanced." Luke pulled back to regard her with a solemn expression. "A man embittered to the point of madness."

She shuddered again. "Yes."

His hand moved to gently cup her face, his sweet breath brushing her cheek.

"He will never trouble you again."

She felt lost in the depth of his blue gaze.

"Where is he?"

"Biddles is hauling him to the magistrate. He will soon be locked in prison."

She slowly released her breath, unable to believe the whole miserable nightmare was over.

"I am safe."

"Yes." An indefinable emotion rippled over the lean features. "You can now go home."

"Home." An unconscious frown marred her forehead.

For so long all she had wanted was to be able to return to Devonshire and resume her peaceful life. It was all that mattered. Now she gazed at the dark features that had become so endearingly familiar and wondered how she could bear to leave.

"That is what you wanted, is it not?"

A curious flare of pain ravaged her heart.

"Of course," she forced herself to say.

"I shall be very happy for you," he said; then his features abruptly twisted with a pained expression. "No. I am lying."

"What?"

"I shall not be happy." His gaze seared over her pale face with a glittering intensity. "I shall be miserable every moment if you are not at my side."

The squalid room, the musty dampness and even her earlier terror faded away as a delicious heat spread through her body.

"Luke —"

"I love you. I adore you." His hand moved to trail over her parted lips. "I want you to be my wife."

He spoke the words that she had secretly longed to hear for days, perhaps weeks, but Cassie warily guarded her heart. She had never thought to fall in love. After her parents' deaths she had been too frightened to open herself up to such loss again. But against her will, Luke had managed to win his way into her affections, slowly stealing her heart. Now she knew she could never be satisfied with his misplaced sense of honor and duty. It had to be love or nothing.

"I am out of danger. There is no more need to protect me."

His eyes darkened, the scent of his warm body surrounding her.

"My desire to protect you was only a portion of why I have forced my way into your life," he confessed, his voice oddly husky. "I had to be near you, because I love you."

"Oh —"

"And from this moment there will be no more forcing. I was wrong," he startled her by saying. "You must be free to make your own choices. And if you choose to return to Devonshire, then I must step aside."

Her eyes widened in surprise. Was this humble man the arrogant stranger who had burst into her life?

"And if I stay?" she asked in soft tones.

She could hear him catch his breath sharply.

"If you stay, then I will never, ever let you go."

A soaring happiness filled her heart. She had come to London to save her home and instead had discovered that home was merely a place to be with the one she loved. She was home so long as he held her in his arms.

"I love you, Luke."

He pulled her tightly against his chest, thoroughly disregarding the impropriety of his behavior. Not that Cassie intended to complain. She was enjoying his embrace far too much.

"And you will marry me?" he demanded, the hint of uncertainty in his eyes touching her heart.

"And I will marry you," she agreed, an impish smile touching her full lips. "But I do not promise to be the most comfortable of wives."

A low, decidedly wicked chuckle filled the room.

"Ah, my beloved minx, I would not have it any other way."

The employees of Thorndike Press hope you have enjoyed this Large Print book. All our Large Print titles are designed for easy reading, and all our books are made to last. Other Thorndike Press Large Print books are available at your library, through selected bookstores, or directly from the publishers.

For more information about titles, please call:

(800) 223-1244
(800) 223-6121

To share your comments, please write:

Publisher
Thorndike Press
295 Kennedy Memorial Drive
Waterville, ME 04901